Dr. Wolf

The Fae Rift Series Book 3

The Four Horsemen

By Cheree L. Alsop

To my loved ones,
It takes a family to write a book,
To dream, to believe, and see it
Come to life.
Thank you for dreaming with me.

To my readers,
May you believe in yourselves,
Dream, and create your own magic.
I believe in you.

THE FOUR HORSEMEN

ALSO BY CHEREE ALSOP

The Silver Series-
Silver
Black
Crimson
Violet
Azure
Hunter
Silver Moon

The Werewolf Academy Series-
Book One: Strays
Book Two: Hunted
Book Three: Instinct
Book Four: Taken
Book Five: Lost
Book Six: Vengeance
Book Seven: Chosen

Heart of the Wolf Part One
Heart of the Wolf Part Two

The Galdoni Series-
Galdoni
Galdoni 2: Into the Storm
Galdoni 3: Out of Darkness

The Small Town Superheroes Series- (Through
Stonehouse Ink)
Small Town Superhero
Small Town Superhero II
Small Town Superhero III

Keeper of the Wolves
Stolen
The Million Dollar Gift
Thief Prince
When Death Loved an Angel

The Shadows Series- (Through Stonehouse Ink)
Shadows- Book One in the World of Shadows
Mist- Book Two in the World of Shadows
Dusk- Book Three in the World of Shadows

The Monster Asylum Series
Book One- The Fangs of Bloodhaven
Book Two- The Scales of Drakenfall

Girl from the Stars
Book 1- Daybreak
Book 2- Daylight
Book 3- Day's End
Book 4- Day's Journey
Book 5- Day's Hunt

The Dr. Wolf Series
Book 1- Shockwave
Book 2- Demon Spiral
Book 3- The Four Horsemen
Book 4- Dragon's Bayne

Chapter One

"Dr. Wolf!"

Aleric looked up to see an orderly sprinting down the hallway.

"Careful," Aleric warned him. "Nurse Talia will scold you for running."

Gregory ignored his remark. "Dr. Wolf! There's a patient with a problem!"

"What is it?" Aleric asked with a hint of humor. All of the patients had problems, otherwise they wouldn't be patients.

"He's frothing at the mouth and biting people. He keeps repeating something about a horse man."

Aleric took off running. Each step pounded through his injured shoulder, but he didn't care. He skidded around the corner and stopped at the sight of the human in the middle of the main E.R. area. Nurses and orderlies surrounded him. The man's eyes were white as though his irises were covered with film. His movements were jerky and he looked from left to right without focusing on anyone.

"Horseman. H-h-horseman," the man groaned.

Froth dripped from his mouth to the floor in great purple glops.

"Let's get you to a bed," Nurse Eastwick suggested.

"Don't touch him!" Aleric shouted.

The hospital staff turned to look at him.

"What's wrong with him?" Nurse Eastwick asked.

"He's seen the First Horseman," Aleric replied. "He's got the plague!"

"When you say plague, do you mean rats, ships, people dying, scarves over mouths, bodies lining the streets type of plague?" Gregory asked.

At that moment, the man chose to spew out nearly a gallon of the purple stuff across the floor.

"I'm taking that as a yes," Gregory said.

"We need to clear the room," Aleric told them.

"Yes, Dr. Wolf. Everybody out of the E.R.," Nurse Eastwick commanded. "Therese, Gregory, take Mr. Jamison and Mr. Franks to Outpatient. They can recover there. Jaroff, instruct Nurse Tarli to take her patient to Recovery as soon as her stitches have been wrapped."

Everyone rushed to follow their orders. Nurse Eastwick eyed the plagued man as though afraid he would start biting people. Fortunately, he appeared quite content to stand there and drip purple froth for the time being.

"What do we do with him?" the nurse asked.

Aleric thought quickly. "If I'm right about the Horseman—"

The man took up the word. "H-h-horseman. H-h-horseman."

"Which I think I am," Aleric said wryly, "Then we have a

huge problem."

"We just got done with a huge problem," Nurse Eastwick said. "Remember the demons? Your shoulder? You're not supposed to be doing anything."

"If you don't want me too…," Aleric said. He walked toward the hallway doors.

"Get back here!" the nurse ordered.

Aleric turned with a grin. "Kidding. Sorry. Not a time to joke. Okay, what do we know about plagues?"

Dartan shoved through the doors Aleric was about to use.

"They're stinky, they like to spread, and there's usually a source." He paused with his gaze on the frothing man. "Like that one."

"Great detective work," Aleric said dryly. "What tipped you off?"

The vampire's lips curled back in distaste. "What I want to know is why you have a plague victim standing in the Emergency Room. You know better than that."

"I didn't bring him here!" Aleric protested.

"I don't believe that," Dartan replied. "All trouble seems to come from you." He pointed at the man. "Trouble." He pointed at Aleric. "You. See."

"I'm offended by that," Aleric said. He tried to cross his right arm over the sling on his left, but it didn't work. He gave up and glared at Dartan. "You'll have to tell I'm offended by my glare because my arm is pretty much useless."

"I'll take your offense at face value," Dartan replied.

"Can we stop arguing and get back to the plague victim?" Nurse Eastwick asked.

Dr. Worthen appeared at the corner. "What's all of this I'm hearing about a plague? I go into surgery, everything's fine. I come out and patients have been relocated, the staff is in an uproar, and should we be concerned about that?" He pointed at the frothing man who had slumped himself over a chair and proceeded to give a loud snore.

"I think it's an improvement," Dartan said.

"Me, too," Aleric agreed. "We need to make a quarantine zone and assume there will be more plague victims rolling in." He looked at the vampire. "I put you in charge of the plague ward."

Dartan's mouth fell open. "Why me? That's not fair!"

"You're already dead," Aleric replied. "So you're not at risk."

The vampire glared at him. "I...am...not...dead," he growled, spacing the words carefully.

"Are you sure?" Aleric asked.

"Yes," Dartan said through his tightly-clenched pointed teeth.

Aleric could hear the vampire's heart pounding, which made the situation all the more hilarious. "Then don't get the purple stuff on you," Aleric suggested. "But if you die, don't worry, you could be a vampire."

Dartan gave an angry huff. "I already am a vampire."

"This conversation is getting nowhere," Dr. Worthen said.

Aleric nodded. "That's where this guy needs to be. Nowhere another patient could run into him. I'm suggesting we turn the D Wing into the quarantine zone until I can figure out where he came from."

"How do you plan to do that?" Nurse Eastwick asked.

"I'll track him. It shouldn't be hard given that he's all foamy and frothy. I'm guessing he left quite the trail."

"You shouldn't go alone," Dartan said.

"The sun's rising," Aleric pointed out. "Your skin's still

healing. I won't confront the Horseman, I just want to find out where he's hiding. You get to stay with Frothy here."

The man burped and a purple bubble popped in front of his mouth.

"Disgusting," Dartan said with a shake of his head. "Why do plagues have to be so ugly?"

"So that everyone doesn't want it," Dr. Worthen replied with a hint of a smile.

Gregory hurried into the room. "Dr. Worthen, Nurse Talia said for me to tell you that the ambulance is arriving with three more plague victims."

"Great," Dartan muttered.

Aleric smiled. "Look on the bright side. The D Wing won't be lonely."

Dartan pointed at the burping, snoring patient. "You call that company?"

Aleric shrugged. "I don't, but I'm not a vampire."

"They can be your pack, Wolfie," Dartan shot back.

A grin crossed Aleric's face. "There it is. Save them for me. I'm sure they'll make an excellent pack."

"At least they won't have fleas," Dartan told him.

"Fleas with the plague. That would spread quickly," Aleric answered. "I'll track Burpy and come back when I'm sure where he came from. The faster we can locate the Horseman, the better."

Aleric made his way down the hall to the back parking lot. He ducked behind the dumpster and pulled off his shirt and sling to phase. It was only when he was in the middle of changing form that he realized what a bad idea it was. The pain to his shoulder was enough to make his breath catch in his throat. He leaned against the dumpster for several minutes telling himself that it wasn't as bad as he was making it out to be. When he took his first step in wolf form, he then told himself that he was an idiot and wounds from silver hurt far worse than they should.

Muttering inwardly about the fact that he couldn't trail in human form, he limped around to the front of the hospital. Fortunately, it didn't take long to find the trail the plagued man had made. The purple globs, which appeared light gray to Aleric's eyes, had a pungent, sulfuric scent to them. It wasn't hard to track from one glob to the next.

Thanks to the early hour, there were few people on the street. Individuals out that early appeared either overly-enthusiastic about exercise and jogged past with headphones on and their gazes distant, or they wore hoodies or big coats and slunk in the shadows as though reluctant to be seen. Those he saw made their way to the other side of the road when they spotted him coming. He gave them the same berth.

The trail took him on a winding course through back alleys and down side streets. It didn't appear as though the plague victim had intended to go to the hospital, he just veered there as the frothing got worse. His steps changed from the indistinct wandering near the hospital to a direct course, solid directions, and a path which led to the front door of a small restaurant.

Aleric backed up a few steps to read the sign. 'Pasta-Pocalypse' was proclaimed in red letters on a green banner across the top of the restaurant. By the scent of the vinyl that wafted down compliments of the early-morning breeze, the sign was new. Aleric could smell flour, eggs, and fresh spinach from beneath the door. After a bit of searching, he located the scent of the patient heading into the restaurant the night before. When he left, the same scent carried with it the faint sulfur odor that intensified the closer he got to the hospital.

Aleric had promised that he wouldn't go inside, and he couldn't exactly phase in public and knock on the door without drawing significant attention to the fact that he had nothing to wear. According to the sign near the door, the restaurant wouldn't be open for another few hours. He checked the back of the building, but despite a few bags of garbage in the alley behind, there was nothing significant about it.

At one moment, near the back wall, Aleric thought he caught the scent of a horse, but when he attempted to find it again, it had vanished.

Frustrated by the lack of information, Aleric took a shorter route back to the hospital. He realized after a few blocks that his left paw, which had been sliced by the Archdemon's silver stake during the fight, was starting to bleed. He gritted his teeth and kept going. He was almost to the hospital when a voice called his name.

"Dr. Wolf! Dr. Wolf!"

The high, small voice made him want to smile, but he smothered the urge with the thought that a wolf's grin looked far too much like a snarl, and the last thing he wanted to do was scare them. He turned at the sound of running feet.

"I'm so glad we found you!" Grimma said.

The six-year-old's arms wrapped around his neck as far as she could reach.

"We have something to show you," Grimsli, her twin brother, told the werewolf.

Aleric didn't want to walk any further than necessary on his bad shoulder. He glanced toward the hospital hidden behind buildings a few blocks away, wondering if he should go change form and then come back.

"Come on!" Grimma urged. "It's important."

Aleric let them lead him toward the alley the grims had

made into a home. Despite the fact that it was indeed just a little closed-off alley between two run-down buildings, the twins had turned it into a cozy place to live. They had been busy since Aleric had seen them last. The cardboard boxes had been stacked to create a cave which was lined with the blankets Aleric had brought them.

Water bottles, the food the werewolf had given them, and small treasures like a Christmas ornament, a cracked hand mirror, several coins, and a lamp that leaned to one side occupied the far wall. A small cupboard that was missing a shelf had been brought in. Two rickety chairs and a ragged rug that looked as though it had seen better days turned the cave into a serviceable room. Aleric was amazed at their scrounging abilities. They would have done as well as he during his days as a Drake City street rat.

The blankets moved. A growl escaped Aleric's throat. He placed himself between the blankets and the grims.

"It's okay," Grimsli said. "That's what we wanted to show you."

Grimma crouched beside him and pulled on the blanket to slide it down. Aleric stared at what was revealed.

An elf lay with her hands clutching her stomach and her eyes shut tight. The silver leaf tattoos along her pale skin revealed that she was a woodland elf whose kind cared for the forests of Blays. Her slender, elegant form was curled around the wound. Aleric wondered for a moment if she was alive, but the faint sound of her heartbeat touched his ears.

Aleric glanced at Grimma.

"We found her near the park," she said. "We heard her crying."

Aleric's gaze shifted to her arm.

Grimma shook her head. "We didn't get her name; I think that means you're supposed to rescue her."

The elf's eyes opened. Her silver irises caught the light from the sun behind Aleric. At the sight of him, her eyes widened in fear and she pushed back against the wall.

"This way," she said to the children. "I'll protect you from him!"

Grimma giggled. "Dr. Wolf's our friend."

Grimsli nodded. "He's here to help you."

The elf gave Aleric a wary look. "Didn't your parents ever tell you not to trust werewolves?"

"He's the one that let us stay here," Grimma told her.

The elf's pained gaze traveled over the twins' cardboard box home. It was obvious by her expression that she wasn't impressed.

Aleric wished he could tell her it was far better than Grimmel's factories.

"Dr. Wolf wants to tell you that it's far better than Grimmel's factories," Grimma said. "And I agree. That place was horrid."

She and Grimsli exchanged a look of horror at the thought of the place they worked before falling through the Rift.

"The werewolf is taking care of you?" the elf asked skeptically. She winced and a hiss escaped her. She doubled over her stomach.

"He is," Grimma said. She glanced back at Aleric. "And he's worried about you. He wants to take you to the hospital immediately."

"A werewolf at...the hospital?" the elf asked between gasps of breath.

"Yes, he works there," Grimma explained. "And he says you're losing blood too quickly."

"How do you know that?" Grimsli asked. "Are you talking to him?"

Aleric was busy staring at the little grim child. The things she said were exactly what he was thinking.

Grimma met his gaze. "Yes, and he's just as amazed about it as you are. You remember how I used to tell you what the birds were saying as they flew past the warehouse? I can hear Dr. Wolf the same way." She giggled.

"What?" Grimsli asked.

"Dr. Wolf doesn't believe me, either," she said.

Aleric gave a snort.

The elf let out a moan of pain. She looked at Aleric with such suffering in her eyes that his heart went out to her.

"Help me, please," she said, her voice weak.

Aleric crossed to her side.

"Dr. Wolf needs us to help her up," Grimma told her brother.

Both of the grims worked together to help the elf half-stand, half-lean with an arm over Aleric's neck. He took several steps toward the mouth of the alley. Her weight made his limp that much more pronounced. He gritted his teeth against the pain and glanced back at Grimma.

"He says to stay here," she told her brother. "He wants us to be safe."

"Alright," Grimsli replied to Aleric. "But if you need our help, howl and we'll be right there."

The thought of having his own little band of rescuers would have been humorous if Aleric wasn't positive he wouldn't need it. With each step toward the hospital, the elf's weight became more pronounced until she was nearly leaning her entire body across his back. Nobody was in sight on the streets to give assistance, though Aleric wasn't sure they would do so if they had the chance. The strange sight of a giant wolf with a slender, bleeding woman across his back would probably evoke fear rather than empathy. Grateful for the thin, tall build of the elven race, Aleric limped through the sliding doors of the Emergency Room.

It took one bark to bring half the E.R. staff rushing into the main room.

"Bring a bed," Dr. Worthen called.

"Prep O.R. Seven," Nurse Eastwick told Therese.

Dartan burst through the doors. "What in Blays?" he exclaimed at the sight of them. "That's an elf."

Aleric rolled his eyes at the vampire's keen ability to point out the obvious. He crouched while the staff lifted the elf onto the bed.

"Is any of that blood yours?" Dartan asked. His face was paler than usual and he kept his distance from them.

Aleric gave a single shake of his head. He watched Dr. Worthen and Nurse Eastwick roll the bed out of sight, then let out a sigh of relief. She was in someone else's hands far more capable than he. A thought occurred to him and he lifted his head quickly.

"I know," Dartan said, raising a hand. "Tell them not to use a saline solution. Elves are allergic to salt. I'll inform them." He hurried after the others.

Aleric didn't want to move. He knew he needed to head back to the dumpster to phase and pull his clothes on, but the thought was nearly more than he wanted to take on. He wondered if he could just stay in wolf form for a few days until his shoulder healed. Perhaps the hospital needed a mascot or a therapy animal. He snorted at the thought and eased back to his feet.

He bowed his head and pushed through the door to the hall at the back of the Emergency Room. He held his left paw up to keep blood from the floor and had limped three-legged halfway to the other door when the sound of familiar footsteps caught up to him.

17

"I thought you looked terrible when you made it to the E.R.," Dartan said. "Now I know for certain. Somebody should remind you that you had surgery yesterday. You should probably act like it. Come on."

Aleric froze at the sensation of being picked up by the vampire and carried into the Light fae section of the D Wing as though he weighed nothing. Dartan let out of hiss of pain when they passed under the UV lights. Aleric wondered vaguely who had rigged them back up after the gargoyles left.

Just when Aleric was ready to protest being carried around like a helpless puppy, Dartan set him on one of the beds.

"Hang on," the vampire told him. "Knowing you, your scrubs are behind the dumpster in the parking lot. You're getting predictable."

As much as Aleric wanted to argue, his shoulder hurt too much to care. He lowered onto his right side and stretched out the aching limb. The action helped to ease the pain somewhat.

The vampire's third intake of breath at the lights heralded his return.

"What did I tell you? Predictable," Dartan proclaimed. He paused when he saw Aleric. "Should I get Dr. Worthen? You look awful."

Aleric snorted and pushed up to a sitting position. He wished Grimma was there to tell the vampire his thoughts, then changed his mind because a child shouldn't have to repeat such things.

At his look, Dartan let out a chuckle and tossed the clothes he held onto the bed. "Get dressed. I'll bring you some food on the pretense of giving you some dignity, although I should point out that you are, for all intents and purposes, completely naked right now. Wolves don't wear clothes. Perhaps that's natural."

Aleric lifted his lips in a mock snarl.

Dartan held up his hands and backed toward the door. "Fine. Fine. Consider me gone. I'd suggest the showers. You got a lot of that elf's blood all over you. At least by the scent, I can tell them what type to give her." There was a tightness around the vampire's eyes that told how the aroma of the blood was affecting him. He opened the door and ducked under the UV lights once more. Aleric heard his hiss of pain.

The inevitable couldn't be put off any longer. Aleric willed his body to phase. He thought of his fingers pressing a bandage to a wound, the sensation of slipping on shoes, the feeling of a shirt brushing against his bare skin. His body changed form. The phase was slow, telling how he had taxed his system. He clenched his jaw so hard when his shoulder shifted and turned outward that his teeth ground together.

The end of phasing found him on his knees gasping for air. He held his shoulder, willing the throbbing to stop.

"I don't have time for this," Aleric muttered. He pulled on his pants and was about to do the same for his shirt when he looked down and realized Dartan was right. He definitely needed a shower. Blood streaked his skin all across his back and side. Putting on the shirt would only force him to find another as soon as he got clean, and Nurse Eastwick already wasn't thrilled about the number of shirts he had gone through since he started working at Edge City Hospital. He glanced out the door, confirmed that the hallway was clear, and hurried toward the staff locker room.

"Can I help you?" a voice asked.

Aleric paused at the sound. He glanced over his shoulder to meet Lilian Worthen's blue eyes. She stood near the corner by the E.R. in a hospital gown with bandages on her arm where she had been bitten by the goblin.

"You're hurt!" she said.

The sight of her made a pit form in Aleric's stomach. He forced a smile. "No. I'm fine. This blood isn't mine." He tried for a joke to lighten the mood. "I suppose this is the one place you hear that all the time."

Lilian's hands went to her hips and she gave him a serious look. "The elf was brought in by a big wolf, so they say."

Aleric gave a half-bow that wrenched his shoulder. "At your service," he replied.

Her eyes widened. "You're a werewolf?"

"Before you believe everything you hear, I don't have fleas," Aleric told her. "Now, if you'll excuse me, I am in dire need of a shower." He paused, then said, "Not because of fleas, because of the blood."

He pushed the door to the locker room open and ducked inside. When the door closed, he leaned against it and shook his head with a sigh. "I'm destined to never have a normal relationship with a pretty girl."

Chapter Two

"I'm going with you."

Aleric jumped when Lilian spoke the moment he left the locker room. He hissed in a breath at the pain to his shoulder.

"Sorry," she apologized, crossing to him. "I didn't mean to startle you."

"Werewolves are supposed to be harder to startle than that," Aleric told her. "I must be out of practice."

She looked him up and down. "You clean up good."

Aleric fought back a smile. "Someone left a pair of

clippers in there. I thought I'd trim up a bit." He ran a hand over his jaw. "It was getting scruffy. Werewolves are scruffy, well, I guess humans get scruffy, too, I don't know." He realized he was babbling. Something about her presence always set him off balance. He noticed what she was wearing. "You're not in a hospital gown anymore."

She smiled at his change of subject. "No, I'm not. Thanks for noticing."

"Well, I just, uh, those gowns get drafty and you're probably more comfortable even though they are comfortable compared to pants because then you're not wearing pants." Aleric let out a breath and pushed his hair back from his forehead with his good hand. "I've got to go."

Lilian repeated what she had said before, "I'm coming with you."

Aleric stared at her. "There's no way your father would approve of that."

She crossed her arms and gave him a straight look. "I'm an adult; I'll make my own decisions."

"He said you were stubborn." The words escaped Aleric's mouth before he could stop them.

Lilian lifted an eyebrow. "He said that?"

"In a nice way," Aleric hurriedly told her. "He was very nice."

"He always is," Lilian replied. She was silent for a moment, watching him. "You're going after the Four Horsemen."

"One of them." Aleric watched her closely. "I think he's the one spreading the plague."

"Then we should find out," she said. "I have a car. I'll drive you."

Aleric shook his head. "Your father would never forgive me if I let you come with me."

"Let me deal with my father," Lilian replied. Her gaze shifted to his shoulder. "Your sling's twisted."

Aleric reached up with his good hand. "I couldn't get it right in the locker room and…." His words died away when she stepped behind him. The feeling of her fingers gently adjusting the straps made his breath catch in his throat.

"Is that better?" she asked.

Aleric tried to speak; he had to settle for a nod and a forced, "Y-yes, thanks."

"Your stitches."

Aleric stared at her, wondering what she was talking about. She pointed to his hand.

"You're bleeding."

He looked at where she indicated. His hand resting in the sling had blood along his palm where the demon had sliced it. He closed his hand before it could drip on the floor.

"Get some gauze on that," Lilian told him. "I'll meet you out front with my car."

It wasn't until Aleric had entered the Emergency Room that he realized he had followed her orders without question.

"What's wrong with me?" he muttered.

"What's wrong with you?" Gregory repeated, appearing from one of the partitions.

Aleric knew telling the orderly Lilian was going with him would very quickly get word back to Dr. Worthen. He opened his hand.

"I'm bleeding."

"Yes, you are," Gregory replied. "Hold on."

Aleric glanced to the left to see a silver car pull up outside the Emergency Room. He looked away quickly.

The orderly returned with gauze. He put a roll of it in Aleric's hand, then wrapped the rest of it around his palm, tying it securely when he was done.

"That should hold things until your magical healing powers take over," Gregory said. "I wish I could heal the way you do. Papercuts would be nothing."

Aleric didn't tell him that wounds caused by silver didn't heal due to a werewolf's allergy to the metal. "Thanks for your help." He glanced out the door. "I'll be investigating the Horsemen, so I'll be gone for a while. How's the elf?"

"The surgery went well," Gregory told him. "Dr. Worthen said he'll be sending her to the D Wing soon. Any instructions while you're gone?"

Aleric nodded. "She should be set up in the Light wing. Please note on her file that she isn't to have saline I.V.'s."

"Already done," Gregory answered. "Nurse Eastwick stamped it as soon as Dartan told her. We're making a list of fae allergies at the nurse's station. It's an interesting one."

"I'll bet," Aleric replied. "Thank you."

Aleric made sure the orderly was gone before he walked out the door. The sight of Lilian waiting for him in her car was an unnerving one. He looked over his shoulder, sure he would find Dr. Worthen there. He wasn't sure how to tell the doctor that his daughter had insisted on going with him to investigate the Horsemen. He doubted his position at the hospital would last very long once the head physician found out.

"Where to?" Lilian asked when he slid onto the passenger seat.

"I'm not convinced this is a good idea," Aleric told her.

"I'm not convinced you could walk there in your shape," Lilian shot back. "Where to?"

Aleric pointed.

Silence filled the car as she followed his directions. Lilian broke it to say, "I've been reading about the Four Horsemen since Dad mentioned them."

"There's literature about them?" Aleric asked in surprise.

Lilian nodded. "They're from the Bible, the symbols of the apocalypse, the harbingers of the last days."

"Sounds promising," Aleric said. He wondered how the Horsemen would feel about the warnings.

A few minutes later found them in front of Pasta-Pocalypse.

"Cute name," Lilian noted.

Aleric climbed out of the car after her. "You'd think the people going in would be a little more wary."

To Aleric's dismay, a line of customers waited impatiently outside. A glance in the wide front windows showed the seats filled to capacity. The sulfuric smell of the plague tingled in Aleric's nostrils when they walked to the front of the line. Many of those waiting stared inside as though they couldn't break their eyes away from the food being served. A few glops of purple showed on the sidewalk near the door where others had already left.

"Wait your turn!" someone called when Aleric opened the front door.

"We're health inspectors," Lilian replied.

They were let inside without a problem. At Aleric's stare, Lilian shrugged. A hint of red colored her cheeks. "I was hoping it would work."

"That was quick thinking," he replied.

"You are out of line." A man with a trimmed mustache and spiked hair glared at them from his podium.

"We're from the Edge City Health Department," Lilian said. She pulled out a card and held it up, then put it away before he could look at it too closely. "We've had complaints from this restaurant, and so we're here to inspect it for compliance issues."

The man watched her for a moment, his mustache

twitching as if he debated whether to believe her. He finally gave a toss of his head and twirled on his heels. "This way."

They followed him to the back of the restaurant. The patrons Aleric passed smelled of the same sulfuric scent. They ate their meals with blank expressions, their gazes empty as they forked pasta into their mouths, chewed, and swallowed with mechanical motions as though they didn't taste it.

"This is creepy," Lilian said. She took a seat at the small table near the back wall the man showed them to. He left without a word.

"Something's off for sure," Aleric replied. "Good job getting us in. That was smooth."

Lilian smiled and Aleric's heart did a backflip. "I just flashed my blood donor card. I didn't think it'd actually work."

A waitress appeared with two glasses of water. "I will bring you the usual," she said.

"We don't get to order?" Lilian asked in surprise.

"There is no ordering," the waitress replied. "You get the usual." She left without giving them a chance to protest.

"This just keeps getting weirder," Lilian murmured.

She lifted the glass to her lips. Aleric noticed at the last minute and swept it out of her hand with his werewolf speed. He set it back on the table without spilling a drop.

At her stare, he said, "I wouldn't eat or drink anything here. Look at them all."

Lilian followed his gaze to the next table. The plates of the patrons were cleaned of all pasta and they stared ahead as though they didn't see anything. A white film covered their eyes and purple drool showed at the corners of their mouths. A moment later, a waiter ushered the barely responsive patrons out of the restaurant and four more took their seats.

"This is straight out of a horror movie," Lilian said.

The waitress returned and placed two bowls of salad and two plates of spaghetti in front of them. The sulfuric smell mingled with a mouth-watering odor that tempted Aleric to try the food.

"Smells delicious," Lilian said. She poked at the spaghetti with her fork. "This did that?"

Aleric nodded. "By the smell of it, yes." He pushed back from the table and stood. "We need to see what's going on in the kitchen. You might need your health inspector's card."

The smile she shot him made his breath catch in his throat. Perhaps braving Dr. Worthen's wrath had been completely worth it.

Aleric led the way through the swinging door and paused at the sight in the kitchen. A man in a white long coat stood behind the lengthy, flat cooking stove. He glowed an other-worldly white from the top of his top hat to his waist; the rest of him was hidden behind the counter. A wreath of glowing green leaves was wrapped around his top hat; by the scent, they were cilantro.

The Horseman looked up at their entrance and his icy blue eyes locked on Aleric. An inadvertent chill ran through Aleric's body. He held the Horseman's gaze for a moment, fighting against the demand of his instincts that told him to attack the threat.

"Dr. Wolf," Lilian whispered. Fear filled her voice and her hand slipped into Aleric's. Warmth combated the cold that had filled his limbs.

The Horseman cleared his throat. His icy gaze narrowed. He opened his mouth, and a hearty laugh escaped him.

"Aleric Bayne! I heard you were here!"

Aleric grinned and met the Horseman halfway across the kitchen. "Perry, it's been a long time." He shook the

Horseman's hand.

"Way too long," Perry replied. He looked over Aleric's shoulder at Lilian. A smile spread across his face at her shocked expression. "I know. Horsemen and werewolves don't usually get along, but this is a rare case."

Aleric turned. "Lilian, this is Perry, the First Horseman."

She held out her hand hesitantly. The Horseman shook it. "You're as beautiful as I'm sure Aleric would have told me if we'd spoken. It's a pleasure to meet you."

"T-thank you," she said. She looked from the Horseman to Aleric. "I didn't know you knew each other."

Aleric lifted one shoulder. "I may have forgotten to mention that. It's been a crazy past few days."

"You said it," Perry told them both. "Crazy things have been happening! One minute we're riding through Drake City and the next thing you know, we're falling down some dark hole. Buffy was terrified when we landed. It took me forever to calm him down."

"Buffy is Perry's horse," Aleric said to Lilian. He turned back to the Horseman. "Where is Buffy?"

"In the back," Perry said. "He doesn't like pasta."

Aleric looked at the pots boiling on the stove. "Speaking of which, there's a few problems with the food you're feeding here, Perry."

The Horseman's eyes widened. "Like what?"

Aleric decided to just tell him straightforward. "Perry, you're spreading the plague."

A hand flew to the Horseman's throat. "What? No! Not here. Aleric, not here. I promise. I would never do anything like that!" His eyes filled with gigantic blue tears. "All I want to do is cook. Is that too much to ask? Yet any time I find a way to fulfill my dreams, something always happens to destroy them." He paused, his mouth open and gaze distant for a moment. His mouth closed with a snap and he dashed the tears from his cheeks. "Fabien."

"What's that?" Lilian asked in an undertone to Aleric.

"Perry's brother," he replied quietly. "The Horseman of Famine." He raised his voice. "You think Fabien had something to do with this?"

"He must," Perry replied. He rushed to the kitchen door and pushed it open. "Look at them! Don't they look like they're starving even though they're eating as if they relish every bite?" He sighed. "And here I thought the line out the door meant they truly loved my food. It's all Fabien's fault."

He grabbed Aleric's good arm. "You've got to help me find him. He'll drive Pasta-Pocalypse into the ground! I can't let that happen. It's my dream!"

"I'll find him," Aleric said. "Just promise me you'll close your doors until we do. We can't have this plague spreading all over the city. I need you to send every patron you have to the Edge City Hospital for treatment. I'm hoping they've figured out a cure by now."

Lilian nodded. "I'm sure with Dr. Wolf's help, your restaurant will be up and running again in no time."

Her words seemed to cheer the Horseman up immensely. Aleric was touched by the way she genuinely seemed to care about the fae's feelings. The smile she gave Perry was warm as though they were good friends, and he smiled back, his eyes bright as if he looked at an angel or one of the luminous elves in charge of painting silver lining on the clouds and sunbursts. Aleric knew how the Horseman felt, because he looked at her the same way. He had thought it was a werewolf thing, but now he wasn't so sure.

He cleared his throat. "We should probably go see if they need help at the hospital. You'll close up shop?"

"Yes," Perry said, nodding emphatically. "I don't want to

spread the plague. You saw what happened in Drake City. If it keeps up, they'll run me out of town."

"We're closing?" one of the other cooks asked. He stopped near Perry's elbow. Several of the other cooking and waiting staff gathered near.

"This is the best place I've ever worked," a waitress said.

"Yes," another cook echoed. "Who knew cooking could be so fun?"

Perry looked at each in turn. "I apologize deeply to you all. You gave me a chance, and I let you down."

A waitress put a hand on his glowing arm. "No, you didn't. You gave all of us a chance."

Everyone nodded.

"We believe in this place," a female cook said.

More nods followed.

"We'll fix the plague problem and make Pasta-Pocalypse stronger than ever!" another cook said.

The watery smile the Horseman gave them made Aleric smile in return. Perry clutched his apron in both hands. "You really want our restaurant to be up and running again?" he asked.

"Definitely!"

"Of course!"

A chorus of approval ran through the staff and flowed among those who crowded in the kitchen doorway.

Perry turned to Aleric. The Horseman put a hand on the werewolf's shoulder. "We're counting on you, Aleric Bayne. Find my brother and help me end this plague so that Pasta-Pocalypse can be up and functioning as a healthy, fun spaghetti restaurant again."

Aleric nodded. "I'll do it. I promise."

Another cheer went up through the staff.

Perry clapped his hands. "First thing's first. Round up

every patron you can and send them to Edge City Hospital." He smiled at Aleric and Lilian. "Edge City's finest will help them recover."

The staff rushed out and began ushering patrons to the door.

"I don't know how I'll ever repay you," Perry said.

Aleric gave the Horseman a worried look. "I don't know how long the city will allow a fae to run a restaurant here."

"I know," Perry replied. "But we've got to try, right?"

Aleric nodded. "We do. I'll do whatever I can to help you keep your dreams."

The grateful look the Horseman gave him filled Aleric with determination. "Thank you, Aleric. I owe you big time."

Aleric walked out the back door with Lilian at his side. They could see a long line of restaurant attendees being helped by Perry's staff toward the hospital. Big frothing glops of purple foam colored the sidewalk.

"Take the back way?" Aleric suggested.

"Definitely," Lilian replied. "We can come back for my car later."

Aleric gave her a careful look. "Are you sure you're up for walking? You just got out a hospital bed yourself."

She smiled at him. "It feels good to stretch my legs. Sunshine is good for the soul."

That brought a chuckle from Aleric. At her questioning look, he explained, "Demons suck souls. Sunshine destroys demons. It's fitting."

She shook her head with a half-smile. "You've had a strange life, Dr. Wolf."

Aleric nodded as he helped her around the overflowing garbage containers behind Pasta-Pocalypse. "You have no idea, and that's probably a good thing."

They reached the other street. A few cars drove past and

a couple walked further up the sidewalk, but it was far less busy than what Aleric was used to seeing. With the sunshine on his shoulders and the plague hopefully under control, he felt the tension easing from him. It didn't hurt that Lilian walked at his side. His ears caught the tune she hummed quietly to herself.

"What song is that?" he asked.

"You heard that?" she replied. The hint of red he loved brushed her cheeks, making the blue of her eyes that much more defined.

"I have pretty good hearing. It's a race characteristic," Aleric said. "I don't mean to pry."

She smiled. "It's something my mom used to sing to me when I was little. It's always in my head. Sometimes I hum it without thinking."

"I'd love to hear it," Aleric told her.

She glanced at him out of the corner of her eye. "I don't sing very often."

"Don't worry," Aleric replied. "I promise I'll be a good audience."

She gave him a shy look, her gaze vulnerable as though she was about to do something she never did. At his reassuring smile, she let out a breath and dropped her gaze. He thought for a moment that she would refuse, then he heard the quiet intake of air filling her lungs.

"Dance in a drop of sunshine,
Spin in the pouring rain,
Skip through the starry meadows,
Remember that life's a game.

Too-ee, Too-loo, Too-ee, Lou-ee
Remember that life's a game.

"Breathe in the scent of flowers,
Run through the morning dew,
Cartwheel through the pansies,
All of life begins with you.

Too-ee, Too-loo, Too-ee, Lou-ee
All of life begins with you.

Smile at the sunlight,
Enjoy the brand new day,
Laugh with the calling birds,
And dance the boredom away."

Too-ee, Too-loo, Too-ee, Lou-ee
And dance the boredom away."

She looked at him out of the corner of her eye. "It's something my mom made up. I don't know why I sing it, really."

"I like it," Aleric replied honestly. "It may be the best song I've ever heard in my life."

She pushed his good shoulder. "Don't tease me."

He gave her a wide-eyed look. "I'm being serious here. Your mother knew what she was doing. That's a great song. It may be simple, but it's happy." His continued, his words a bit quiet, "The more happiness in the world, the better."

Her expression became one of surprise. "That's what my mom always said."

"She was a smart woman," Aleric concluded.

Lilian nodded. Her voice was quieter when she said, "Yes, she was."

Her tone gripped Aleric's heart. The sadness resonated

inside him. "I lost my mother when I was four."

He didn't know why he said it, but there was something about seeing Lilian sad that made him want her to understand she wasn't alone.

"I didn't know that," she replied. "I'm sorry to hear it."

Aleric nodded. "She was a very loving person."

"You miss her," Lilian said.

He nodded again. "Every day. I always will. She is who I think about when I think of love and safety."

"And your father?" Lilian asked.

Aleric toyed with a string that frayed from the edge of his sling. "Not so much," he said quietly.

"My father was the opposite," Lilian said. At Aleric's glance, she explained, "Before my mother passed away, he was always at work. I barely saw him. He was so involved in his job, and I couldn't blame him. Even when I was young, I knew he was saving lives. That was very important to all of us. But when Mom got in the accident, he changed completely. He did what he could to be both mom and dad for me. I don't know what I would have done otherwise." She looked at him. "What did you do?"

Aleric thought of his father beating him over and over the days before his mother died. His dad had blamed him for his mother's sickness, even though Aleric had nothing to do with it. Aleric knew now that his father hadn't coped well with the thought of losing his true love. Werewolves never handled that well.

"I ran away," Aleric admitted.

Lilian stared at him. "How old did you say you were?"

Aleric pulled on the string. The hem near his hand unraveled. "Four," he said without looking at her.

"That's horrible!" she exclaimed.

Aleric didn't answer. He kept his focus on the string he

pulled, watching the seam unravel while his thoughts were on another life in a different time.

Lilian put her hand over his, stopping his fingers. Both of them quit walking.

"You're unraveling it," she said.

He met her gaze. Her face was inches from his own. He felt like he was falling into the depths of her beautiful blue eyes. It was ridiculous, and he knew it. He had only known her for hours, maybe, if everything was totaled; yet in that moment he understood why his father had lost his mind at the thought of saying goodbye to the one love in his life. For the first time, Aleric truly understood.

But she wasn't a werewolf. There was no way Lilian could understand the way a werewolf's heart worked. For her, as a human, there was no true one person, no immediate connection, no point where she would be unbreakably drawn to him the way he was to her.

Aleric gave a small cough and looked away. "We'd, uh, better get back to the hospital."

"Yes," she said, her words quiet past the thundering of his heart. "Yes, we should."

They started walking again. They were almost to the corner when a man came running out of the apartment building ahead. He looked around frantically and spotted them.

"Diablo!" he shouted. "Diablo! In my kitchen! Come help!"

Aleric and Lilian took off running.

Chapter Three

"Stay behind me," Aleric said as he crept through the man's small living room toward the kitchen.

"It's by the stove," the man said from the doorway to the hall. His voice shook with terror. "It's a devil for sure."

Aleric peered into the kitchen. He couldn't see or smell anything that had set the man off. He looked around, his senses straining. The only thing he smelled was the peanut butter sandwich that sat untouched on the table, and a faint hint of cat.

"What is it?" Lilian asked in a whisper.

"I'm not sure," Aleric replied. "I think—" A slight scratching sound caught his attention. Something between the stove and the counter was making it. "Hold on," Aleric told Lilian.

The werewolf crossed the rug on silent feet. His ears picked up the sound of Lilian following close behind despite his command. He reached the edge of the counter and peeked over.

A small black creature looked up at him from where it was wedged between the back of the stove and the corner of the counter. Big golden eyes blinked at him and a small sound escaped the creature's mouth.

"Diablo!" the man yelled from the living room. "Save yourselves!"

The sound of him running back into the hallway was loud in the small room.

"You've got to be kidding me," Aleric said under his breath.

"What is it?" Lilian asked.

Aleric knelt next to the stove. The space was narrow. He had to wedge his good shoulder against the counter and force his arm into the crack. He gritted his teeth against the pain the strain brought to his silver wound.

Soft fur brushed his fingers. He reached further. Sweat broke out across his forehead at the pain. Aleric clenched his jaw and leaned in.

"Gotcha," he said as his fingers slipped to the back of the creature's neck. He pulled. The creature didn't fight when he drew it forward through the crack.

"Here's the diablo," he said, holding it up. The tiny black kitten gave a pitiful meow. Aleric turned it to reveal the black wings held tight to its back.

Lilian's hand flew to her mouth. "What is it?" she asked, her gaze filled with compassion.

"A minky," Aleric replied. "A winged cat. They swarm Blays once in a while, usually in the spring. It's amazing how much trouble a flock of these can get into."

"It's so cute!" Lilian exclaimed. She held out her hands. "Can I hold it?"

Aleric deposited the creature in her hands. The little minky looked at her with its large golden eyes and it gave another tiny meow.

To Aleric's dismay, the scrawny kitten launched itself off Lilian's hands and landed on his chest, clawing his shirt to avoid falling.

"Ouch!" he exclaimed as its claws pierced his skin.

Lilian helped him work its claws free, but as soon as she lifted the minky clear, it scrambled back into Aleric's arms. Before he could protest, it nestled into the crook of his good arm and started to purr.

"You've got to be kidding me," he muttered.

Lilian gave a light, musical laugh. "She likes you!"

"I don't like her," Aleric replied. He tried to lift the minky clear, but it latched onto the sleeve of his scrubs with all sets of claws. "Minkies don't like werewolves," Aleric protested.

"She seems to think otherwise," Lilian pointed out.

"D-did you get the devil?" the man called from the hallway.

"We've got it," Aleric replied.

He and Lilian crossed to the door. Aleric thought that maybe seeing the minky outside of the corner might calm the man's nerves, but when he appeared in the hall, the human cowered against the wall with his fingers held out in a cross in front of him.

"Diablo," he cursed. "A devil in my kitchen. Destroy it!"

"It's just a little—"

"Keep it away from me!" the man shouted, cutting Lilian off. He inched around both Lilian and Aleric and ran for his door. He slammed it behind him. Aleric heard him mutter, "Evil Diablo. Mangy flea-bitten devil."

"That's not what I expected," Lilian said.

"Me, either," Aleric replied.

He realized the minky had moved. During the commotion caused by the human, the kitten had relocated itself to the inside of Aleric's sling. She now rested on his arm that was held against his chest. The tiny creature gave a meow and closed her eyes, her wings held loosely against her back.

"This is not happening," Aleric said.

"What?" Lilian replied. "She's cute!"

Aleric gave the human a straight look. "She's a pest."

Lilian reached a hand into Aleric's sling and ran a finger across the kitten's little head. A purr emanated from the fae.

"Stop it," Aleric said. "You're encouraging her."

Lilian smiled up at him. "You secretly like it."

"I hate it," Aleric replied. "It's nasty and horrible."

"She's adorable," Lilian coaxed.

Aleric couldn't keep his annoyed front up in the face of her teasing. He followed her adoring gaze to the little creature that had attached itself to him.

"I guess she's kind-of cute," he admitted.

Lilian gave him a look of triumph. "I knew you had a soft-spot."

Aleric shook his head. "I don't. At all. It's hideous."

She laughed as she followed him back outside. "You have a good heart."

"I do not," Aleric denied. "Don't start saying that. You'll ruin my reputation."

She tipped her head at him. "You have a reputation?"

Aleric nodded. "I'm heartless and mean."

Another laugh broke from her. "I don't believe you for a minute, and neither does the minky."

They walked along in the sunshine, its warmth on their shoulders and a smile on both of their faces. They were nearly to the hospital when a thought occurred to Aleric.

"I have a stop to make. Come with me."

Lilian looked surprised. "I thought you were worried about my father."

"If he's going to kill me, I'd better prolong this for as long as possible. Besides, I have a promise to fulfill."

Lilian followed him into the convenience store. Aleric roamed the small aisles where he had made his first purchase in Edge City. He selected the biggest block of cheese he could find in the refrigerated section.

"Do you want bread with that cheese?" Lilian asked.

Aleric shook his head. "Just cheese." He grabbed a box of bars and another of crackers that were also cheese flavored.

"You must really like cheese," Lilian noted.

"Something like that," Aleric replied.

"Empty the register!"

Aleric's muscles tensed at the angry words. He glanced to the right over the rows of goods. The sight of two men with guns standing near the front counter sent adrenaline through Aleric's body.

"Here," he said quietly to Lilian.

Aleric was relieved when the minky didn't protest being handed to the human. He drew off the sling and set it on a shelf with the items he had found.

"D-don't shoot," the cashier, a man in his late fifties dressed in a green shirt bearing the store's name 'Truman's' begged. "I don't have m-much. You took it last time when you shot Theo."

"Shut up and empty the register," the man closest to the counter barked. He pointed to the small stack of grocery bags. "Put it in there."

"I think you should leave."

Everyone turned at the sound of Aleric's voice.

"Dr. Wolf, what are you doing?" Lilian asked in an undertone. A glance behind him showed that her face was pale. She held the minky close.

"Stay here," Aleric told her.

He crossed toward the men. "You need to leave, now."

Both men turned their guns on Aleric.

"Or else what?" the first man asked. "You planning to be a hero? You don't have any weapons. What's to keep me from shooting you right now?"

"The fact that if you do, one bullet won't be enough to kill me. I'll will hunt you down and tear you to pieces," Aleric replied calmly.

The man glared at him. "I'll shoot you, your girlfriend, and this guy. I don't care."

"You're not going to shoot anyone," Aleric said.

"Try to stop me," the man replied. He leveled his gun at the cashier, his finger tight on the trigger.

Aleric pulled off his shirt and phased. The moment his paws touched the floor, a growled rolled from his throat, reverberating off the walls and shaking the windows.

"W-what is that?" the man closest to the door asked.

Tiny claws dug into Aleric's shoulder. He glanced up. The little minky gave a hiss from her perch, her wings spread and tiny teeth showing.

The first man backed away from Aleric. "Get out of here!" he shouted to his comrade.

They both burst out the door. The men took off down the street so fast the first one tripped on the curb. The second pulled him back up and they darted around the corner out of sight.

"D-don't hurt me," the cashier pleaded.

Aleric met the man's gaze. His face was washed pale, his eyes wide, and his fingers shook as he clutched them in front of his chest in a pleading gesture. The fear drove straight to Aleric's heart with the force of a dagger. He glanced to the right and found the same fear on Lilian's face. Her eyes were wide and terror was easy to see in the depths of her blue gaze. The look hurt more than Aleric had thought it would.

He grabbed his scrubs shirt and pants in his fangs and limped around the end of the aisle. Grateful for the adrenaline that dulled the pain in his shoulder, Aleric willed the change to come. He thought of the sensation of gravel beneath his shoes and the feeling of scrubbing his hands in the O.R. sinks. Willing his heartbeat to slow, Aleric remembered the soft brush of Lilian's fingers against his neck when she adjusted the strap of his sling.

The phase pulled at his shoulder when the bones rolled back, repositioning themselves for his human form. Aleric bit back a gasp at the pain. He crouched, leaning against the shelves for a moment. His bandages were long gone and the flesh of the wound was red and raw where Dr. Worthen had burned it. Aleric opened and closed his left hand. His fingers moved sluggishly and the gash along his palm pulled against the flesh. It felt as if his ability to heal quickly as a werewolf warred against the silver that had caused the wounds. It wasn't a pleasant feeling.

Aleric pulled on his pants. He worked his shirt gingerly over his shoulder and glanced up. His heart slowed. In the corner of the small convenience store was a convex mirror to show what was happening within the aisles. His eyes locked on Lilian's from where she waited with the minky in her arms near the cashier. The thought that she had seen him at his weakest, hunched over in pain, bothered Aleric. He dropped his gaze and pulled on his shoes.

Aleric reached Lilian's side and maneuvered the sling over his head. She moved to help him, but he turned away and eased his arm inside the mesh. She wordlessly held up the minky; the kitten settled in his sling once more.

Aleric grabbed the bars, cheese, and crackers from the shelf where he had set them during the confrontation and placed the items on the counter.

"You're that Dr. Wolf," the man behind the cash register said. He looked calmer now as if whatever he and Lilian had spoken of while Aleric dressed had calmed him. "You're from the hospital!"

"You saw me on television?" Aleric asked. He had seen the fear on the man's face when he phased. The fact that he was willing to talk made Aleric grateful for the reporters who had put his actions on their stations.

The man nodded quickly. "Several times. I saw that you were a good man; now I know for sure."

That brought a smile to Aleric's face. "I'm glad you think so."

"I know so," the cashier replied. When Aleric attempted to pay, he waved his hand. "It's on the house. You saved me money and probably my life. Anything you want here is yours."

"I can pay," Aleric replied. "Really. You don't have to do that."

"And you didn't have to risk your life for a stranger," the man told him. He held out a hand. "I'm Truman. This is my store." He placed the items Aleric wanted into a bag. "Whatever you need, you take. I won't accept payment. My wife would kill me if I charged the man who saved my life for anything."

Touched by the man's gesture, Aleric picked up the plastic sack.

"What if they come back?" he asked.

Truman smiled. "Did you see the looks on their faces? I'd be amazed if I see them for a very long time."

"Good," Aleric replied. "If they do come to bother you again, let me know."

"Gladly," Truman replied.

Aleric walked down the street in silence. Mixed emotions filled him at the sound of Lilian's footsteps following behind. He didn't speak and she seemed to respect his silence. He had seen the fear on her face when he changed into a wolf. He couldn't blame her; a huge wolf in the place of a man was terrifying, especially when one wasn't used to such a thing. A part of him wanted to ask her what she was thinking, but the other side noted that he was probably better off not knowing.

When he took a street a few blocks from the hospital, he caught Lilian's curious look. "Where are we going?"

"I have a promise I need to keep," Aleric replied shortly.

He paused at the mouth of the alley near the hospital and looked at her. "You can wait here if you prefer."

"I'll come," she replied.

Aleric entered the alley. It was quiet. He crouched, listening to the sound of two bated breaths within the cardboard boxes. The grims had found several more to cover the front of their roughly-made home and disguise it. Aleric approved of their additions.

"It's Dr. Wolf," he said. "I've brought a friend."

Silence met his words.

He continued with, "I brought cheese."

The boxes flew apart and the two six-year-olds appeared eagerly in front of Aleric. He heard Lilian's breath catch.

"Grimma, Grimsli, this is my friend Lilian," he said. He turned to find that she had crouched beside him. There was a kind smile on her face that made Aleric's heart give a double-beat. He willed it to calm.

"Hello," Grimma said.

"Pleased to meet you," Grimsli echoed.

"It's good to meet you both," Lilian told them.

Their cat-like eyes kept straying to the bag Aleric held. He opened it and pulled out the block of cheese. "I keep my promises," he told them.

Grimsli gave a yip of excitement and watched as his twin sister eagerly took the cheese from Aleric's hand.

"I brought you some more bars and some cheese crackers as well," Aleric told them.

The twins took the food from him and were about to return to their cardboard house when the minky gave a little meow.

"What was that?" Grimma asked.

Aleric pulled the minky from his sling. "Meet Diablo," he told the children.

Lilian gave a little laugh at the name.

"It's so cute!" Grimma gushed. She handed her brother the cheese and rushed back to Aleric. "Can I hold it?"

Aleric gave the kitten to her. Grimma ran her fingers over the creature's silky black fur.

"She's so soft," the grim said. She touched the feathers along the kitten's wings.

"Maybe she can stay with you," Aleric suggested.

Grimma giggled when the kitten rubbed its head against her chin. "That would be fun!"

Relieved he didn't have to worry about the minky anymore, Aleric rose to his feet.

"Is there anything else you guys need?" he asked Grimsli.

The boy shook his head. "We're happy here."

"It's supposed to rain tonight or tomorrow," Lilian said. "My dad has an old tent we don't use. I could bring it to keep the rain off of you."

"That would be amazing!" Grimsli replied.

Aleric gave Lilian a grateful smile. She smiled back.

"I'll see you both later," Aleric promised. "I'll bring some more water."

"Thank you," Grimsli called from inside the cardboard house.

"Bye, Dr. Wolf," Grimma said.

Aleric was nearly to the mouth of the alley again when Grimma gave a little squeak. He looked back to see the little minky galloping toward him across the asphalt. Meows sounded from the tiny animal and her wings flapped as she pushed herself faster.

Diablo reached Aleric and scaled up his pants. Her sharp claws dug into his skin as she pulled herself back up to his sling and climbed inside. She settled on his arm once more. A moment later, a contented purr emanated from the kitten.

"I think she wants to go with you," Grimma said.

"I don't need a minky," Aleric protested.

Diablo gave a loud meow.

Grimma giggled. "I don't think you have a choice."

Aleric looked back at Lilian. "Help me here," he pleaded.

She shook her head with a laugh. "I think Grimma's right. Diablo's picked you."

Aleric gave a dramatic sigh and everyone laughed.

"Fine," he said. "But as soon as this sling's gone, she's going to leave me. She's just comfortable."

"You tell yourself that," Lilian told him.

"Come on, Grimma," Grimsli called from inside their little home. "I've got the cheese open."

"Coming," Grimma replied. She dove into the boxes.

"Catch you guys later," Aleric called out.

The only sounds in reply were chewing and laughter from inside the boxes.

Aleric and Lilian had walked a block when she said, "You're a surprising person."

Aleric glanced at her. "Is that a good thing?"

She nodded. "Definitely." She met his gaze. "I guess I didn't know what to expect."

Aleric couldn't read her tone. "From the big bad werewolf?" he asked.

"From the man who saved my life," she replied.

Aleric turned his gaze back to the sidewalk in front of them. Vehicles rushed by without care for the pedestrians that walked beside the road. Many of those Aleric and Lilian passed barely glanced at them; a few, upon seeing Aleric's scrubs, did a double-take. He heard one man whisper, "Was that the guy from Channel Five?"

"Where I'm from, most people don't trust werewolves," Aleric admitted after a few minutes had gone by.

"Why?" Lilian asked. "There must be a reason for that." She gave Aleric a questioning look.

He walked several more steps before he said, "In Blays, the fae are divided into Light and Dark. The Dark fae generally either don't like the sun or are physically unable to survive in sunlight. The Light fae fear darkness because of those who roam it." He studied the pattern of the bricks that made up the building beside them. "Werewolves are called Ashstock, one of the few races who are in between because of our animal side, like the grims." He glanced at Lilian. "The other fae fear us because they wonder if we're more animal than man."

"Are you?"

Lilian's question hung in the air between them.

Aleric let out a breath. He could lie. It would be easy to pretend to forget the past. Yet those days had a lot to do with who he was, and for some reason he couldn't explain, it felt important to him that she know that.

"Sometimes," Aleric said. He appreciated the way she gave him time to gather his thoughts.

They passed a mother and father with two blond, curly-haired boys. The boys stared at him as they walked by and Aleric heard them whisper, "That's him!"

Aleric's thoughts went to other little boys living in alleys together, struggling to survive, fending for each other like the mismatched pack they were.

"Can I show you something?"

Lilian's question caught him by surprise. Aleric nodded.

"Come this way," Lilian told him.

She led the way between the rows of apartments just before the hospital. Aleric followed her down two blocks to a wooden fence. Lilian looked around, then pulled up a loose slat and ducked inside. Bemused by her actions, Aleric reached his fingers through the slats and followed. The minky in his sling gave a little meow at the unexpected movement. Aleric straightened on the other side of the fence and paused.

Flowers and vines wove a tapestry of beauty within the small, sunlit garden. Rose bushes taller than Aleric showed every color of rose imaginable. Lilian had disappeared from sight. Aleric followed the small rock pathway between the bushes. It turned to the left to reveal a circle of flowers with a bench in the middle. Lilian met Aleric with a shy look from her seat on the bench.

"I've never shown anyone this place before, not even my dad," she admitted.

"Why show me?" Aleric asked her.

Lilian watched him, her gaze searching. "I'm not really sure. I guess I felt like you needed it." She patted the bench beside her. "Just like you need a break. Come join me."

Aleric sat on the stone bench. The silence that fell around them was comfortable like the sunshine. Lilian didn't rush what he was going to tell her, and he appreciated her patience.

"I found this place shortly after my mother died," Lilian said. She ran her fingers along the petals of a rose that grew near the bench. "I spent a lot of time at the hospital because my father was still busy and there wasn't much for a little girl to do. He hated when I wandered, but I couldn't help myself." She waved her hand. "When I found this garden, I began to sneak away here all the time." She smiled. "Mrs. Fadden, who owns the house, found me back here once. When I told her about my mom, she said I could come here whenever I wanted."

"That was nice of her," Aleric replied. He bent gingerly and picked up a twig. When Diablo gave a meow of protest, he said, "Oh hush, freeloader." He straightened and she settled in the sling again. A quiet purr resonated from her.

Aleric studied the twig. "I wished I'd had a garden like this to go to when my mom died." He thought about it. "That's the answer to your question, really. When I ran away to live in the streets of Drake City, I was four years old, without any survival skills, and at the mercy of anything in the city that wanted to either eat me or put me to work, which was pretty much everything." Aleric snapped the twig between his fingers. "I found that people were far more likely to give a starving wolf pup scraps than a street urchin, so I stayed in wolf form. I eventually found others hiding out and we joined together. I'd beg for scraps, others would steal, and we'd pool our findings so we could all survive."

49

"No wonder you care for those children in the alley," Lilian said.

"Children need someone they can count on," Aleric replied. He snapped the pieces of the stick. The movement hurt his injured hand, but he didn't care. "Sometimes it was easier to just be a wolf, to be an animal, to pretend that I wasn't one of those people who could just walk by in the streets and ignore children who were supposed to look to adults for protection and love. I couldn't understand it."

He looked at her and found compassion and sorrow in her gaze. "I've never told this to anyone."

"I'm glad you told me," she replied. "It's got to be hard to be so far away from home."

Aleric slipped his hand into the sling and petted the little kitten. Its purr rose until the creature practically vibrated. "This feels more like home than that ever did." The admission caught him by surprise. If anyone had told him he would be bearing his soul to Lilian in a secret garden in the middle of Edge City, he wouldn't have believed them. He gave her a self-conscious glance. "That's enough about me. We'd better get back and see to the plague victims."

Lilian rose with him. She followed him to the fence. Before he could push through the slats, she stopped him with a hand on his good arm. It took a surprising amount of strength to meet her gaze after all he had said. When he did, the compassionate smile on her face filled him with warmth.

"I'm glad you trust me. I promise to keep your secrets."

"They're all I have," Aleric replied.

Her smile deepened. "I don't believe that."

That brought a smile to Aleric's face as well. He ducked under the slat and held it up.

"Thank you," she said when she rose.

They made their way in amiable silence to the hospital.

Aleric glanced at Lilian. "As much as I like to tangle with death, I think it'd be better if we pretend like you didn't just meet the First Horseman."

"Agreed," Lilian replied. "I'll sneak around back, but only to save you from Dad's wrath."

"I appreciate it," Aleric told her.

She walked to the back and waved at him before she disappeared around the side. Her scent, a mixture of jasmine and sunshine, lingered in the air. It was hard for Aleric to turn away. He did so with a shake of his head and walked toward the Emergency Room. Aleric's instincts tingled, setting him on edge by the time he reached the doors. Inside, he found nurses and orderlies scrambling.

Aleric caught Gregory's arm. "What's going on?"

"The EMTs are on their way with a patient," Gregory replied breathlessly, "But the patient attacked them. Dr. Worthen said to prepare for the worst."

Chapter Four

"The patient attacked them?" Aleric repeated. "Like with a knife?"

"Claws," Nurse Eastwick said. She reached them with a wheeled stretcher. "That's all we could hear, someone shouting out 'Watch for the claws!'"

A siren caught Aleric's ears. "They're coming," he warned them.

Dr. Worthen appeared from the other end of the room. "Bring the other two stretchers and be ready; according to the last transmission, the patient is still actively hostile."

"Let me go first," Aleric said, walking beside the doctor.

"There's no way," Dr. Worthen replied. "You just underwent surgery last night. I don't even know why you're up."

"The patient has claws," Aleric repeated. "I'm going first."

Dr. Worthen looked like he wanted to argue, but he glanced behind him at the waiting nurses and orderlies. The doctor was in charge of the safety of each individual in the waiting room. None of them knew what was coming. He gave in with a nod. "Fine. But Dartan's on his way here with the stun gun. If the patient's hostile, let him shoot it."

"Gladly," Aleric replied.

The ambulance sped up to the E.R. so quickly Aleric feared it would crash through the glass doors. The driver slammed on the brakes at the last moment and the vehicle careened to a halt. Aleric rushed out with the rest of the staff close behind. He reached the handle of the back door with his good hand and pulled. The door swung open.

A rumbling snarl filled the air. The hair stood up on the back of Aleric's neck. He stared at the blood and destroyed equipment inside the ambulance. Three EMTs cowered behind the overturned bed. On the other side, a creature with slick, tawny fur crouched. When he met Aleric's gaze, his tufted ears flattened on either side of his human head. His arms ended in huge feline paws tipped with massive black retractable claws. Ragged canvas pants were the only clothing the creature wore. His cat-slit eyes narrowed.

"What is that?" Gregory breathed behind Aleric.

"A sphinx," Aleric replied without breaking his gaze from the fae's.

Another snarl tore from the sphinx at the sound of Aleric's voice. The sphinx's tail twitched from side to side in the small space. Its muscles twitched.

"Look out!" Aleric shouted.

He ducked as the creature launched itself over them. The sphinx darted into the Emergency Room and slid on the tiled floor. Aleric followed close behind. The big cat-creature spit at him and swiped its lethal claws. Aleric jumped back before it opened his stomach.

"Can we talk about this like civilized beings?" Aleric asked.

The sphinx wrinkled his human nose. "You stink of werewolf, Ashstock."

"And you smell like the Glass District. Missing the sand?" Aleric replied.

The cat spit at him again.

A tiny hiss sounded in reply. The minky's head stuck out of Aleric's sling. She bared her teeth and hissed.

The appearance of the kitten seemed to catch the sphinx off guard. He rose onto his hind legs like Aleric was used to seeing. The change from wild animal to hopefully civilized person was reassuring.

"Why are you carrying a minky?" the sphinx asked, his eyes not leaving the kitten.

"I rescued her," Aleric replied. "And she's refused to leave me despite my encouragements."

That brought a hint of a wry smile to the sphinx's curved lips. "A werewolf with a minky. I never thought I'd see the day."

"Me, either," Aleric replied.

At the corner of his periphery, Aleric could see the doctor and nurses scrambling to help the EMTs from the ambulance. For the moment, the sphinx was distracted, but if he became upset again, everyone in the E.R. could be in danger.

"Why did you attack those humans?" Aleric asked.

The sphinx glanced behind him. His golden eyes narrowed. "I awoke strapped to a table."

"They were trying to help you, not hurt you," Aleric explained.

"How do you know?" the sphinx shot back.

"Look at them. Do they look dangerous to you?"

Aleric followed the sphinx's gaze, careful to keep an eye on the creature.

"Not really," the sphinx said. Confusion colored his tone. "Then why did they trap me?"

"They don't know the dangers of cornering creatures like us," Aleric replied. "We're not from around here."

The sphinx looked around quickly. His sharp gaze lingered on the glass that was unmarked by sand wisps and the walls that didn't bear the crest of the forest dwarves. Aleric knew the absence of the footsteps of the cotton pixies was noticeable on the curtains hanging around the partitioned rooms.

"We're not," the sphinx stated. He took several steps backwards. "So where are we?"

"Edge City," Aleric replied. "There's more to it than that, but before we get into it, I need you to let the EMTs come in for treatment. I can't allow them in here if you're still a threat."

The sphinx looked outside once more. Dr. Worthen had the three EMTs on the beds. Nurse Eastwick and Nurse Talia were doing the best they could to bind wounds with the bandages they had brought with them, but it was clear at least two of the EMTs needed more care. The ambulance driver held bandages on his forearm and waited with Gregory near the beds.

"I did that." It was more of a question than a statement.

There was horror in the sphinx's voice.

"You were cornered," Aleric told him. "But they didn't know any better. Humans don't react the way we do."

The sphinx's eyes narrowed. "We are not the same."

Aleric gave him an exasperated look. "Have it your way. But let them in. If they die out there, it's on your head."

To his relief, the sphinx nodded.

"Come in!" Aleric shouted.

Dr. Worthen stepped forward and the door slid open. Aleric kept carefully between the sphinx and the staff as the nurses and doctor wheeled the EMTS past.

Dr. Worthen gave Aleric a short nod. Aleric hoped the confidence the head physician placed in him did not come back to bite him figuratively or literally.

The ambulance driver followed behind the others. He was almost clear when Aleric heard familiar footsteps.

The back door to the E.R. flew open.

"Revenant," the sphinx growled. He launched himself at Dartan.

The vampire lifted the stun gun and shot three darts into the sphinx. The creature hit the ground unconscious a foot from the vampire. Dartan and Aleric stared at each other.

"Making enemies?" Dartan asked.

"He hated me before he got here," Aleric replied.

"Cats and dogs," Dartan said.

Aleric rolled his eyes. "It's a bit more complicated than that."

"How so?"

Aleric opened his mouth to reply, then shook his head. "Fine. Cats and dogs. But he was under control until you got here."

"I could tell," Dartan said dryly. "I could smell the blood from the D Wing."

Aleric glanced behind him. "I have to go see if they need help. Can you handle the cat?"

"He'd kill you if he heard you call him that," Dartan pointed out.

Diablo meowed.

Dartan tipped his head to one side. "Did I just hear a kitten? Don't tell me the sphinx came with a litter."

Aleric reached into his sling and pulled out the minky. "I found this little devil striking terror in someone's apartment."

Diablo worked free of Aleric's grip and climbed up his arm. She rubbed her head against the side of his face and purred.

Dartan cracked a smile. "He likes you."

"She," Aleric corrected, trying to get her down. The kitten sunk her claws into his shirt and refused to move. "And I don't have time for her."

"Is that what you tell all your women?" Dartan replied. "Oh, wait. You don't have any. I think I know why."

Aleric rolled his eyes at the vampire. "Can you take her to the D Wing?"

"I don't think that'd be a great idea," Dartan replied seriously. "It's full of plague victims. We're keeping them somewhat happy with Nurse Eastwick's concoction of antibiotics and electrolytes, but it's a mess back there. She'd be better off with you, and I don't say that lightly."

"I can't help patients with a minky hanging around," Aleric told him. "How about the Light wing?"

Dartan accepted the kitten. "Fine." She scrambled, trying to sink her claws into his skin. "Whoa little one. You don't want to get on my bad side." The smile he gave the minky let Aleric know the kitten would be just fine. The vampire boosted her onto his shoulder. "Hang on there and I'll find you a spot until Uncle Wolfie gets back."

Dartan ducked under the sphinx's arm and pulled the creature up on his other shoulder with his vampire strength.

"Come on, Claws," Dartan said, pushing through the back door. "If I have to shoot you again, I won't be sorry about it."

"I appreciate it," Aleric called through the door.

"You better," Dartan replied.

Aleric hurried through the room in the direction the others had gone. He followed the scent of blood to the Operating Rooms.

Gregory and Therese waited near the doors.

"How are they doing?" Aleric asked.

"Dr. Worthen and Dr. Brooks have Tom in surgery. His stomach was torn open pretty good," Gregory said. "Nurse Eastwick is in stitching up Anderson's thigh while Nurse Talia preps Jenna."

"What about the driver?" Aleric asked.

Therese nodded to O.R. Seven. "Jaroff's waiting with Ulrich. Dr. Russell's been paged."

"You guys are organized," Aleric noted with amazement.

Gregory nodded. "We're prepared for emergencies like this."

"Don't let him say it," Therese told Aleric.

"Say what?" Aleric asked her.

"Do you know why?" Gregory pressed.

"Don't let him say it," Therese repeated.

Aleric looked from Therese to Gregory. "Uh, why?" he asked.

"Because it's the Emergency Room," Gregory replied with a triumphant grin.

Therese threw her hands up in the air. "It's not funny when you've heard it a thousand times," she complained.

"Dr. Wolf's only heard it once, right, Doc?" Gregory

asked.

Aleric nodded. "That was the first time."

"It won't be the last," Therese muttered.

Gregory grinned. "My day is made."

Aleric looked past them at the closed rooms. "Will you let me know if they need me?"

Gregory nodded. "Immediately."

"You look tired, Dr. Wolf," Therese noted.

Aleric smiled. "No rest for E.R. doctors, right?"

"Now you sound like Dr. Worthen," Therese said. "When was the last time you ate?"

"You sound like Nurse Eastwick," Aleric told her.

Therese smiled at him. "I take that as a compliment. Go to Minnow's. We'll call you there if Dr. Worthen needs you."

The thought of relaxing at a restaurant sounded amazing. "Where is it?" Aleric asked.

"Follow your nose," Gregory said. At Aleric's look, he grinned, "Two blocks south, one block west. You can't miss it."

Aleric eyed the open back door of the ambulance when he walked by. Blood showed on the floor and the overturned bed. He hoped the EMTs would be alright.

It was a strange position in which he found himself. He very much wanted to be in the Operating Rooms helping with the surgeries, yet he wasn't actually a doctor. His experience with fae had granted him a minor role at the hospital, but in times where only humans were injured, his expertise didn't help at all.

Aleric's frustrations at being unable to assist Dr. Worthen faded when he rounded the corner outside. The scent of Minnow's filled his nose with mouth-watering aromas. Gregory was right; Aleric could have found his way blindfolded. He pulled open the front door of the small restaurant and a smile spread across his face.

The sight of the diner booth seating, the wide windows, and a waitress moving between the few occupied seats felt like he had stepped into a movie. Aleric knew places like Minnow's existed in Drake City, but he had never been to them. The fact that he had his own money, could order whatever he wanted, and take his time to enjoy it felt like a gift.

The waitress walked up to him with a smile and twinkling green eyes. Her nametag read 'Iris'. "Table for one?" she asked. Her blonde curls bounced on her shoulders when she tipped her head invitingly.

Aleric nodded. "Just me."

"Right this way, cutie," she told him. She offered him a seat near the window. "Will this work for you?"

Aleric gave her a smile which she quickly returned. "Anywhere would be perfect. This is great." He slid into the seat.

"I'll be back with some water unless you'd like to order a different drink," she said.

"Water would be great," Aleric told her. "Also, I may be in a rush. Is it possible to put in an order for a chicken cordon bleu sandwich?"

"Of course," she replied. "I noticed the scrubs. We get quite a few of the hospital staff here. I imagine it gets busy over there."

"It's a little crazy," Aleric said, working to keep the weariness out of his voice.

"We don't often have doctors in slings," Iris said.

Aleric glanced down. "Minor surgery. No big deal. This is just a precaution."

"I'm glad to hear it," she said. "I'll go get your water and put in the order for your sandwich."

When she was gone, Aleric eased his arm out of his sling. He stretched it out on the table. The ache in the joint was persistent. It throbbed when he put his hand his shoulder and attempted to massage it. He ducked his head, concentrating on easing the pain.

Fingers touched his hand and he froze.

"Relax," the waitress said from behind him. "My sister's a masseuse; she's taught me a few things. Maybe I can help."

Aleric lowered his hand slowly. Iris kept her touch gentle. She started at the top of his shoulder and slowly, carefully, worked down the outside of his arm. She reached his mid-bicep and went back to the top, then kneaded gradually down the front of his shoulder.

Aleric's muscles tensed the closer she got to the aching wound. He tried to relax.

"Right here?" she asked.

Aleric nodded. His jaw clenched in preparation for the pain, but instead of massaging, Iris felt the edges of the wound gently through his scrubs. He saw her brow crease out of the corner of his eye. Her other hand went to the back of his shoulder and she traced the same edges.

"This isn't from a minor surgery," she said quietly.

"No, it's not," Aleric admitted.

Her touch was soft as she carefully massaged the muscles leading up to the wound but kept away from it. Under her care, Aleric felt his shoulder relax. His eyes closed at the lessening of pain and a sigh escaped his lips.

"That bad, huh?" she asked with empathy in her voice.

He realized Iris had stopped massaging. She stood to the side of the table watching him. Embarrassed that he had gotten so comfortable under her touch, he sat up and eased his arm back into the sling.

"It's a lot better," he told her. "You have a healing touch.

Thank you."

She smiled down at him. "My pleasure. I'll go get your sandwich."

He realized she had set the glass of water in front of him. He took a long drink, then sat back.

Iris returned a few minutes later with the sandwich and French fries on a plate. She set a second plate next to it.

"Our famous mudslide pie," she said. "Your meal's on the house."

"I planned to pay," Aleric replied. "I brought money."

She smiled at him. "Dr. Worthen from the hospital saved the life of Minnow's owner, Reanna, when she got in a bad car accident. Reanna and Dr. Worthen's wife were both in the same accident." She lowered her gaze. "His wife didn't survive."

Aleric realized Iris was talking about the accident in which Lilian's mother had been killed.

"That must've been hard on him," he said.

Iris nodded. "Reanna feeds the E.R. staff for free. She knows she doesn't have to, but she wants to. It's her way of saying thank you for the fact that she was able to see her three boys grow up."

"That's very nice of her." The scent of the food was making Aleric's mouth water.

As if the waitress guessed it, she winked at him. "I'll let you eat in peace. Just call my name if you need anything."

"Thank you, Iris," Aleric replied.

By the time he made it to the hospital again, Aleric felt full and at peace. The moment he entered the back door, the feeling vanished. The sounds of commotion that came from the D Wing let him know something wasn't right. Aleric burst through the door to the Dark fae side and stared.

The plague victims were no longer the catatonic beings

that had been led to the hospital. Every part of the room was filled with quarreling, fighting, biting, spitting, punching, angry humans.

"Dartan?" Aleric called out.

All of the plagued turned at the sound of his voice. The closest human let out a garbled yell and they surged forward.

Aleric grabbed a tranquilizer gun from where Dartan had hung them near the door. Grateful to see that it was loaded, Aleric fired as fast as he could. Small red-tufted darts hit the chests and necks of the plague victims. As soon as one fell unconscious to the ground, another took its place.

Aleric jumped up on the closest bed and dodged to the left, firing as he leapt from bed to bed. More plague victims collapsed to the ground. Aleric fired one last dart and the gun was empty. He immediately regretted the path his flight had taken. The humans surged forward, clawing at his feet and knees as he pressed as far back against the corner as he could without upsetting the bed on which he stood. Instincts pressed at the back of his mind, urging him to phase and protect himself.

He knew he could fight them. He doubted they could do much damage to him in his wolf form, armed with fangs and thick fur to protect his hide, yet that would also mean going on full attack and injuring those who weren't aware of what they were doing.

Hands grabbed Aleric's scrubs and pulled him forward. He kicked them away, but more took their place. Aleric had nowhere to run. Frothing mouths gnashed teeth and filmy white eyes stared at him; the victims let out moans and grunts that set Aleric's teeth on edge. He had no other choice. There was no way out but through the humans.

Aleric slipped his sling over his head and was about to phase when the doors burst open.

"Aleric!" Dartan shouted.

The vampire carried two tranquilizer guns in his waistband. He drew them out and shot from the hip, taking down the plagued and reloading so fast Aleric could barely follow the speed of his reflexes.

"Over there!" Aleric called out, pointing to two of the humans who crawled toward Dartan despite their darts.

Two more darts hit home and the humans collapsed.

"Behind you!" Dartan shouted.

One of the plagued had worked his way behind the bed on which Aleric stood. At Dartan's shout, the man grabbed Aleric's ankles and yanked backwards. Aleric fell to his chest on the bed. The bed tipped over when the man pulled again. Aleric fell to the ground and rolled. The plagued man bit at him over and over. Fortunately, Aleric's sling prevented the man's teeth from breaking his skin. Aleric shoved his injured arm up, trapping the man against the wall.

"Duck!" Dartan shouted from behind him.

Aleric ducked and held his arm over his head for protection. A thwack sounded. The plague victim fell to the ground with a heavy thud.

Aleric dared a peek over his sling. The room was silent. He lowered his arm to find Dartan grinning at him from beyond the overturned table.

"You didn't know vampires made such good cowboys, did you?" Dartan asked.

Aleric let out a sigh of relief. "I had no idea, but I'm grateful."

Dartan made a show of spinning the tranquilizer guns around his fingers before he shoved them back in his waistband.

"They started getting out of hand, so I ran for Dr. Worthen's office. Gregory mentioned that the other tranquilizer guns had arrived and I knew we didn't have enough darts to stop them all in here," the vampire said.

Aleric stared around the room at the fallen humans. "What made them get so riled up?"

"I'm not sure," Dartan replied. "But I have an idea."

Aleric met the vampire's gaze. "War," they both said together.

Aleric shook his head. "If the Third Horseman wants to start a riot, he sure found a good way to do it. If we can track down Famine, maybe he can lead us to his brother."

"Good idea," Dartan told him. "It's still daylight, so I'll leave the tracking up to you."

Footsteps caught Aleric's ear. He hurried through the bodies to the door. He opened it just as Lilian pulled open the main doors into the D Wing.

Chapter Five

"Hello!" Lilian said with surprise in her voice at Aleric's sudden appearance.

She tried to look around him inside the Dark fae side, but Aleric pulled the door shut behind him. The last thing he wanted was for Lilian to meet Dartan. According to Gregory, it seemed all the vampire needed to do was speak to a woman and she fell for him. Aleric at least wanted a chance, and given Dartan's track history, Gregory might be right.

"Is everything alright?" Lilian asked. "I thought I heard something strange."

"Everything's fine," Aleric replied. "Dartan made a mess, but he's cleaning it up." He walked toward the door where Lilian stood, giving her no choice but to back up into the hallway.

"I heard that!" Dartan shouted.

"What did he say?" Lilian asked.

"I'm not sure," Aleric said with a smile. "I think he said he had it under control."

"Oh, good," Lilian replied. She pointed toward the outside door. "It's getting stormy. Should we go get the tent for the children in the alley?"

Aleric nodded. "That's a good idea. But they're grims, not just children."

"Is there a difference?" Lilian asked.

Aleric gave her a searching look. "You noticed the cat eyes and the strips on their skin, right?"

She nodded. "Of course, but they are also children. They need someone to watch after them."

Aleric opened his mouth to argue, then realized he had been doing exactly what she said, looking after the grims so that they would have an easier time in their youth than he had experienced. "Yes, you're right," he gave in.

"We need to get the car from Pasta-Pocalypse, so I guess we're in for a walk," Lilian said.

"I don't mind walking," Aleric told her. "It's the driving that scares me."

She chuckled, realized he was completely serious, and burst out with a laugh that must have surprised her because she covered her mouth. "How is that possible?" she asked. "This city is terrifying, even for me and I grew up here. You never know who you're going to run into out there." She pushed open the door and waited for him to pass through.

He gave a one-shouldered shrug. "Well, I can guarantee

one thing."

"What's that?" she pressed.

"There's nothing out there as terrifying as me," Aleric told her.

She gave a little snort of humor and fell in beside him. With the sunlight on his shoulders and Lilian at his side, Aleric decided he could walk forever along the streets of Edge City. He didn't mind the traffic, whether it was the many, many vehicles or the pedestrians that either ignored them both completely or gawked when they recognized him.

If he wasn't careful, he was more likely to get his shoulder run into as to meet a kind smile, but he found he enjoyed the anonymity that came with being just another face in the crowd. It was a different sensation than Drake City. In Blays, most of the fae citizens had either an acute sense of smell, a great memory, or an inherent distrust of those around them. Aleric was used to being regarded with disgust, fear, or loathing depending on where he was. In Edge City, for the most part, unless his scrubs made him catch someone's attention, he was ignored like the majority of the crowd around them. It was nice, in a chaotic, jostled around, seen through instead of looked at kind-of way.

"It's strange to see it without the crowd," Lilian said, breaking Aleric's musing.

He looked up to find that they were across the street from Pasta-Pocalypse.

"It's better than seeing hordes of plague victims ingesting their poisoned meal," Aleric replied.

"All the same, I'm sad for Perry. He's much different than I thought the First Horseman would be."

That brought an amused smile to Aleric's face. "What did you expect?"

"I don't know," Lilian replied as they crossed the street.

"Scary, I guess. I figured heralding the beginning of the Apocalypse would look a bit less, well," she pointed at the sign, "inviting."

"Fire and brimstone," Aleric guessed.

She nodded. "Death, destruction, and all that."

Aleric walked around to the other side of her car. "You haven't met Perry's brothers yet."

"Are they that bad?" she asked as she unlocked the door.

Aleric was about to reply when a truck caught his attention. The side of the vehicle said 'Quality Ingredients Brought to a Restaurant near You, Courtesy of Barnaby Farms.'

"Wait a second," he told Lilian.

He left the car and heard her fall in behind him as he made his way down the alley where the truck had turned. It backed slowly ahead of him, its driver intent on steering carefully between the buildings on either side.

"What are you doing?" Lilian asked.

"Well, we know Fabian is poisoning Perry's food so that his restaurant fails," Aleric replied. "What we don't know is where to find Fabian."

Lilian's gaze lit up. "So we find out which ingredient is poisoned and follow it to the Second Horseman. That's brilliant!"

"My question is why is Perry receiving a food shipment when the restaurant is shut down?" Aleric mused.

"There's one way to find out," Lilian replied. She reached for the backdoor of the restaurant near the loading dock and pulled on the handle. It refused to budge. "Well, that was underwhelming."

Aleric bit back a smile. "Let me try." He tugged on it, found it locked, and put some of his werewolf strength behind turning the handle. It gave a sharp snap and turned.

"How did you do that?" Lilian asked in amazement.

Aleric shrugged. "I think you loosened it."

They both went inside the dark restaurant. The sound of voices guided Aleric's steps. They drew near to the kitchen in time to hear a door creak open.

"Thank you for this." Perry's words resonated down the hallway. "I know I owe you, and I promise I'll make good on my payments as soon as the restaurant is up and running again."

"Don't worry," a thin voice answered. "My family can't get enough of your pasta. Keep feeding us and I'll make sure Barnaby keeps sending fresh vegetables. I've never tasted spaghetti so close to the way my mom used to make it."

"I'm just glad we figured out what the problem was," Perry replied. "I hated fearing the spread of plague to my patrons. Fabian will be upset when he finds out."

"I'll take care of Fabian," Aleric said, entering the kitchen.

"Aleric! Lilian!" Perry exclaimed. "I was hoping we'd see you again soon!"

The Horseman walked over and shook both their hands.

"Good to see you, too," Aleric replied. "So you figured out where the contamination was coming from?"

Perry's gaze went back to the tall, extremely skinny man near the door. He stood with a dolly in one hand. His back was hunched and the look he gave them was a shy one as though he wasn't used to addressing strangers. He had bright orange eyes that stood out in his very pale face. His fingers were long and thin from arms that looked as though they were merely bones wrapped in skin. His clothes hung on his skeletal frame that was far taller than any human Aleric had met. Lilian's hand touched Aleric's when the thin man's gaze met hers.

"It's alright," Aleric told her in a whisper. "He's a

slenderman from Blays. He won't hurt you."

"Tell them, Reginald," Perry said.

The slenderman ducked his head, a habit that seemed to come naturally given his hunched form. "Well, it's, uh…." He cleared his throat and glanced at Perry.

The Horseman took pity on his friend. "It's alright. You don't have to be afraid of Aleric. He's a werewolf, but he's a good sort. It's the tomatoes," the Horseman explained. "Reginald started dumping the tomatoes he brought from Barnaby Farms and picking some up from the market instead. It seems to have fixed the problem."

"Are you sure?" Aleric asked, watching Perry closely. "You've been feeding it to people? Hold on."

He walked up to the slenderman near the door. Reginald took a step back in surprise. Aleric held up a hand. "Trust me. I'm a doctor."

He could hear Dartan's laughter in the back of his head. The vampire would definitely have gotten a kick out of the line.

Aleric walked slowly around the slenderman. Though Reginald stood still, his head swiveled to follow Aleric more than halfway around, then turned back the other way to continue the same. Aleric sniffed carefully, checking for any sign of the sulfur scent that would herald the plague. He wondered if he should phase to wolf form to be extra sure, but given the slenderman's terrified gaze and ready-to-flee posture, he figured he was pushing it as it was.

Satisfied, Aleric looked back at Perry. "I don't smell any sign of the plague."

Both the Horseman and Reginald let out a sigh of relief.

Aleric gave Perry a steeling look. "What were you thinking? You risked this man and his family. You can't play around with lives like that."

The Horseman lowered his gaze. "I'm sorry, Aleric. I can't help it." He looked up. "All I want to do is feed people. If I'm not doing that, than why am I even here?"

"You mean in Edge City?" Lilian asked.

Perry's expression was one of sorrow when he shook his head. "I mean here at all, in existence. Doyle says we're all here for a reason, but he's Death, so he could just be saying that for the irony of it."

"The Fourth Horseman's name is Doyle?" Lilian asked in an undertone.

Aleric fought back a grin. "Scary, huh?"

"Anyway," Perry continued, "I thought when we fell through the Rift that this would be my chance to start over. I have a reputation in Blays as Pestilence, which doesn't exactly say, 'Come try my manicotti. It's to die for.' I'm afraid people will take that literally or Doyle will. He has a sick sense of humor." The Horseman pushed his top hat further back on his head. The white glow around him seemed dimmer than before given his melancholic state. "I just wanted this to be different." His voice lowered. "Maybe I should go back to Blays."

The ache Aleric heard in Perry's voice resonated with the werewolf. He felt the same way about his position at Edge City Hospital. Given his own experiences in Blays, working as a fae doctor was like a breath of fresh air, a new chance to start over at life without the prejudices and assumptions that had followed him anywhere he went in Drake City.

"We'll make it work."

Everyone looked at Aleric. He kept his eyes on the Horseman. "Perry, I know how important this is to you. We'll get to the bottom of the plague, I'll have a talk with Fabian, and we'll open up Pasta-Pocalypse to the public again so that you can make your dreams come true."

"You mean that?" the Horseman asked with a hopeful expression.

Aleric nodded. "I do. Just please, try to abstain from cooking until we can ensure that the contamination is gone completely. I'm worried War might be involved with this as well."

Perry stared at him. "What does the plague have to do with Wallace?"

"The victims at the hospital are starting to attack the staff," Aleric explained. He noticed Lilian's horrified expression. "That's what you heard in the D Wing. We got them all tranquilized and Dartan's getting them settled." He fought back a chuckle at the thought of the mess he had left the vampire in. At least he didn't have to worry about Dartan drinking their blood. Even the vampire wouldn't risk catching the plague.

"Wallace and Fabian did take off together when we found ourselves here," Perry said. He crossed his arms in front of his chest and glowered at the air in front of him. "I can't believe they're both working to destroy my restaurant." He shook his head. "They just can't let me be happy, can they?" He looked at Lilian. "Try having a brother whose entire goal in life is to cause chaos and uprisings. It makes for some pretty interesting family dynamics."

"I can't imagine," Lilian replied. She set a hand on the Horseman's arm. "We'll get to the bottom of the plague so you can open your restaurant again." She gave him a reassuring smile. "Dr. Wolf and I will be your first patrons when you reopen."

"You're a saint," Perry told her. "And that's saying a lot coming from one of the Four Horsemen. We know our saints. I will prepare the most amazing meal for you that'll make all other pastas pale in comparison." He held out a glowing white arm. "And I know pale."

She laughed and gave him such a warm smile Aleric felt a glimmer of jealousy that he immediately snuffed out.

"Thank you, Perry. I'm looking forward to it."

Lilian nudged Aleric.

"Oh, me too. For sure," Aleric replied. He looked at Reginald. "Could you give us directions to Barnaby Farms? If the tomatoes are contaminated, that'll be the best place to start."

"I'm heading that way right now," Reginald replied. "Y-you're free to follow me if you promise not to eat me."

Aleric stared at him. "Eat you?"

"I told you," Perry said. "Werewolves may have had a bad reputation in Blays, but Aleric's one of the good ones." He winked at Aleric. "The only good one, in my opinion. He doesn't even like the taste of slendermen."

"That implies that he's t-tried them before," Reginald said.

Aleric realized everyone was watching him and waiting for a reply. He held up both hands, which was difficult with his sling. "I've never eaten a slenderman, honest," he said. "I don't know how this conversation landed at this point, but I prefer my meat cooked and preferably of the farm variety."

"He said 'preferably'," Reginald whispered in an undertone to Perry. "That implies that there are other options."

"I can hear you," Aleric replied. "It's one of the perks of being a werewolf."

"I don't trust him," Reginald whispered again despite Aleric's words.

Aleric heard Lilian smother a laugh. He shot her a look that said Reginald's fear wasn't funny. She attempted not to smile and failed entirely.

She finally put a hand on the hunched slenderman's arm. "Reginald, I'll vouch for Dr. Wolf. He's a good guy and he's only trying to help."

The slenderman looked as though he wanted to argue, but it seemed Reginald couldn't in the face of Lilian's plea. He finally gave a small smile. "Alright, ma'am. I'll trust you." He shot Aleric a glare. "Not him, but you. I'll show you where the Second Horseman is."

"I sure appreciate it," Lilian replied. She gave Aleric a triumphant look.

He fought back a smile at her teasing and followed her through the restaurant.

"You'll let me know when it's safe to open again?" Perry called from the kitchen.

"I'll let you know," Aleric replied.

"You promise?" Perry pressed.

"I promise," Aleric said before he left through the door.

He slid into the car, grateful that he didn't have to try his hand at driving in the crazy city again.

"It's kind-of sweet, don't you think?"

Aleric looked at Lilian. "What is?"

"The Horseman. He cares so much about feeding people. It's sweet." She pulled onto the road after the Barnaby Farms truck.

"He was spreading the plague. I don't know how sweet that is," Aleric replied.

He looked out the window as they drove past Pasta-Pocalypse. He could see Perry sitting at a table with his head in his hands and his top hat on the table. Even the Horseman's glow had a dejected cast to it.

"It's sweet that he's so passionate about it. It's obvious how much it means to him," Lilian replied. "How nice would it be to feel so certain about your path in life?"

Aleric stared at her. "His path is one of the Four Horsemen. You said it yourself. He's a bringer of plagues and pestilence, whether Fabian had anything to do with this or not. He heralds the Apocalypse."

Lilian was quiet for a moment before she said, "Pasta-Pocalypse."

That brought a laugh from Aleric. Lilian laughed as well. When she quieted, she glanced at him. "So are you saying that a person can't go against their nature? From what it sounds like, that's what you're doing."

Her words caught Aleric off-guard. He watched the buildings pass out the window. They were smaller on the outskirts of the city. Soon, long stretches of land took off interspersed by small houses and barns.

"You're right," he said into the silence.

"I shouldn't have said that," Lilian replied. "I'm sorry."

Aleric shook his head. "It's true. Everything you've heard is true. Reginald's fear is well-founded. Werewolves are volatile and will protect each other no matter who stands in their way. They work for the good of the pack."

"But you don't have a pack here," Lilian said, her words quiet.

"I didn't have a pack there, either. Not after the other werewolves were killed," Aleric said. "I'm used to being a lone wolf."

The silence that settled between them bothered Aleric. He cleared his throat. "Sorry. I don't know why things got so depressing."

"You don't have to pretend like everything is fine," Lilian replied. At Aleric's glance, she continued, "It can't be easy, all of this." She waved behind her to indicate the busy part of the city they had left. "I can't imagine waking up and finding myself in some strange city surrounded by demons and who knows what else is out there trying to kill me."

Aleric gave a half-smile. "The demons are the normal part."

A little laugh escaped from Lilian. "I'm starting to see your problem."

That caught Aleric's attention. "And what's that?"

"Demons aren't normal, Aleric."

A smile spread across his face that he couldn't keep away.

"What are you smiling about?" she asked. "Loreen told me you got a stake stabbed through your shoulder by a demon and it almost killed you."

"That's the first time you said my name," Aleric replied. "Dr. Wolf's just a silly title I haven't even earned. Sometimes it's nice to just be me."

Lilian looked at him a moment before she turned to face the road again.

"By the sound of things, you've earned the title, Aleric."

The fact that she went out of her way to say his name again wasn't lost on him. Aleric sat back in his seat. "I just happen to know more about fae than your father and he gave me a chance because of that." He was quiet for a moment, then said, "He was kind to me. In Blays, werewolves are judged the moment they are found out; they're treated with hostility and fear. You saw it on Reginald's face; that's how it was every day of my life since I was four."

Aleric looked out the window. "But your father didn't do that. He may have been afraid at first when I showed him what I was, but he trusted me and he treated me with the same respect I used for him. I've never had that before; I stayed because I wanted to repay that."

He saw her look at him out of the corner of his eye.

"Dad doesn't expect repayment," she said.

Aleric nodded. "Just the same, I'm staying."

A hush settled between them. Lilian broke it to say, "I'm glad." At Aleric's questioning look, she indicated the truck in front of them. "How else am I going to have the chance to search out the Four Horsemen and save plague victims, cure the outbreak, and perhaps halt the coming of the Apocalypse?"

A chuckle escaped Aleric. "That does sound pretty amazing. Now I have to stay."

Lilian laughed.

Chapter Six

Lilian followed Reginald's directions past the many warehouses and crops of Barnaby Farms. She guided the car down a dirt road with weeds growing high enough in the middle that they scraped the bottom of her car. The sun was setting through the gray clouds that had gathered above, making a moody counterbalance to the waving strands of wheat and stalks of corn that stretched toward the darkening sky. Several raindrops splatted on the windshield.

Lilian turned the car down the barely-noticeable path that led through the trees. Small leaves clung to the branches and shook in the evening breeze. The trees loomed over the path, their white branches reaching and intertwined. "This is creepy," she noted.

Her car hit a deep hole and Aleric gritted his teeth against the jolt to his shoulder. "Maybe we should walk from here."

She nodded. "Good idea. It looks like it only gets worse."

Aleric took a deep breath by habit as he climbed out of the car. A scent touched his nose amid the atmosphere aroma of the storm. His instincts thrummed. Steel ran through his body and a familiar pit formed in his stomach. "Hold on," he said.

Lilian paused at his tone. Aleric looked around quickly, but there was nothing to see in the bushes between the trees. The evening light cast a strange glow in the air. Aleric checked the breeze again. The scent had vanished.

"What's wrong?" Lilian asked.

"Something's out there," Aleric replied. "Something Dark fae. But I can't smell it anymore."

If Lilian thought him using smell as a warning was strange, she gave no sign of it. She fell in at his side and walked with him along the path.

"How's your shoulder feeling?" she asked.

"It doesn't bother me if I don't breathe," Aleric replied.

Lilian cracked a smile. "That good, huh?"

Aleric bent down to pick up a stick. When he did so, the scent caught his nose again. His stomach twisted.

"Wait," he said.

Lilian stopped. Aleric took a few steps forward. The odor grew stronger.

"We're in trouble," Aleric said.

He slipped his sling and shirt off, ignoring the pain brought by speed. Before Lilian could ask what was wrong, he stood in wolf form in front of her, his teeth bared and ears held flat against his skull.

Two creatures left the shadow of the trees. Aleric heard Lilian gasp. He couldn't blame her.

The male gorgons slithered forward; their snake forms wriggled across the grass and weeds with barely a sound. They towered over seven feet tall, arching high on their snake bodies. Each had a double set of arms sprouting from the torso, and their human heads contained the slit yellow eyes of snakes. Their only article of clothing was a dark cloak fastened around the neck to protect their sensitive spines from attack.

The closest one smiled at their fear and his forked tongue darted out from between his needle-like fangs, fangs Aleric knew contained the poison for which the gorgons were feared in Blays.

"Seemsssss we have found the Ashsssssssstock," the gorgon said.

Aleric had never fought a gorgon before. They were muscular and quick; tales of their merciless poison and the ability to slowly crush the bones of their victims with their snake bodies were told in Blays. Though Aleric had shared his fair amount of encounters with the Dark fae, he avoided them whenever possible. Yet with Lilian at his side, there would be no running away. Two gorgons against one werewolf was a losing battle, but one Aleric was prepared to fight. He bared his teeth and was about to growl when Lilian surprised him by stepping in front of him. She hefted a branch from the side of the trail.

"S-stay back!" she demanded, her tone loud to almost hide the quiver of fear in her voice. "I won't let you hurt him!"

Aleric felt as surprised as the gorgons appeared. No one expected the young woman to react with fight instead of flight. A surge of respect for Lilian's bravery filled Aleric.

"No sensssssssssse in being foolisshshshshsh, girl," the gorgon said. His tongue slid out again as he tasted the air.

The other slithered to the left. Aleric kept an eye on both of them, looking for a chance to catch the gorgons by surprise. It was his only hope to protect Lilian.

Rain pattered to the ground around them.

"I won't let you lay a hand on him," Lilian threatened.

"Try to sssssssssstop ussssssss," the gorgon hissed.

It surged forward.

Aleric darted in front of Lilian. He leapt at the gorgon. His attack caught the creature off-guard. Aleric grabbed the gorgon's throat in his teeth and used his momentum and weight to drive the creature to the ground. He tore out the gorgon's throat with a shake of his head. Aleric left the body writhing on the ground.

Lilian struggled to keep the second gorgon at bay with her branch. The gorgon snapped at her arm. His fanged mouth shut millimeters from her flesh when she slammed the branch against the side of his head.

Aleric reached the pair before the gorgon could retaliate. He bit at the creature's back through its cloak, but the thick fabric kept his fangs from penetrating its skin. The gorgon reached around and grabbed him by his ruff. The creature slammed Aleric to the ground. The pain that coursed through Aleric's shoulder stole his breath. The gorgon leaned down to bite him.

Fear of the poison and the pain it would bring urged Aleric to run, but the gorgon held him tight. The creature's fangs glittered with dark liquid as it opened its mouth. Its fingers entwined in Aleric's thick fur. It pulled the werewolf up to its face and was about to bite down when the branch slammed across the back of the Dark fae's head.

Aleric dove out of the gorgon's grasp. Lilian hit it across the face again so hard the gorgon fell backwards. Aleric was on it in an instant. He grabbed its musky flesh in his fangs and tore the reptilian skin with his sharp incisors. Blood gushed into the grass at his paws. He looked around quickly.

He had killed two of the deadly creatures. Aleric knew consequences would follow. Gorgons were minions of Dark fae he had thought he was done with. Their presence said he had not left them far enough behind.

Aleric stepped back in time to see three more gorgons leave the trees. Whoever had sent them through the Rift to search for him wasn't messing around. Pain from his shoulder pushed at the back of Aleric's mind, but adrenaline surged through his body, keeping the worst of it at bay.

The rain fell harder.

"What do we do?" Lilian asked.

Aleric glanced up at her. Her face was pale and her hands gripped the branch so hard her knuckles showed white. Rain dripped through her hair and down her face. The fear in her eyes ate at him. He wasn't about to let anything happen to her. The gorgons were after him. There was only one thing he could do.

Aleric took off running for the trees. He passed the gorgons and heard all three of them turn to follow.

"Aleric! Wait!" Lilian called.

Aleric ran faster, drawing the gorgons away from her. The first gorgon's words echoed in his head. 'We have found the Ashstock.' They had been looking for him. If he was their target, the least he could do was draw them as far away from Lilian as possible. The only problem was that gorgons were far faster than they looked.

A tail hit Aleric's side so hard he crashed into a tree. As soon as he fell to the ground, Aleric pushed up to his paws and darted around the trunk. Another tail hit the tree with such force that branches and leaves rained down. The gorgons surged around the trunk. Aleric backed up, attempting to keep all three in sight. The gorgons slithered to each side. Aleric felt a prickling of fear as they surrounded him. He kept his gaze on the one in front.

"Don't fear usssssssss," the gorgon said.

"It'll only hurt for a ssssssssssecond," another hissed.

"Yesssss," the third gorgon echoed. "Only a ssssssecond."

Aleric flattened his ears against his skull and let out a growl.

The first gorgon's mouth opened. His hinged jaw elongated, spreading so wide Aleric's entire head could fit in the snake man's mouth. "We were hoping you'd sssssssssay that," the gorgon hissed.

All three of the gorgons attacked.

Aleric dove a split-second before they reached him. The gorgons on either side collided. Aleric darted to the right of the gorgon in front of him, spun at the last second, and slammed his good shoulder into the gorgon's. The creature fell to the ground. Aleric knew he had to take out at least one of them to have a chance. He lunged forward with his teeth bared to deliver a killing blow when another gorgon grabbed his back. The creature's fingers latched onto his fur. He was hauled off his feet.

A searing pain struck Aleric between his shoulder blades. Warmth coursed through his muscles, flowing and writhing like fire. Paralysis followed wherever the poison flowed.

"Fight that, little Ashsssssstock," the gorgon said.

Aleric twisted in the Dark fae's grasp and bit deep into the gorgon's arm.

The creature let out a yell and threw Aleric across the

clearing. The werewolf slid to a stop on his side. The gorgons slithered across the grass toward him. It took all of Aleric strength to reach his paws again. He limped forward through the rain, determined to go down fighting and take as many of them with him as possible.

They attacked in a mass, swarming him and pinning him down beneath their writhing bodies. Aleric felt teeth sink into his back and sides. He bit back, tearing musky flesh and hearing the answering yells. As the poison sank in, Aleric felt his body struggling to change back to human. It was an Ashstock's defense, phasing back to regular form in one last-ditch effort to fight back. The paralysis flooded through his limbs, making his movements sluggish.

A head snaked past his face. Aleric shoved with his legs and grabbed the creature's neck in his teeth. The gorgon reeled back, pulling Aleric with him. The werewolf bit harder. The gorgon fell backwards. Aleric snapped the creature's neck between his jaws.

The werewolf tried to run, but his legs wouldn't respond. A gorgon grabbed him and wrapped him in its long body.

"You're finishshshshshshed," the gorgon hissed.

The coils tightened. Aleric let out a yelp of pain at the crushing sensation to his shoulder. He tried to move, to bite, to claw, to do anything to get out of the gorgon's grasp, but the poison was sinking in. His limbs wouldn't respond. Though his instincts screamed for him to fight back, Aleric couldn't do anything as the darkness closed in on his mind.

He looked up to see a face loom above the gorgon's. White teeth showed in the moonlight before they sunk into the gorgon's neck. Aleric couldn't breathe. His eyes closed despite him fighting to keep them open. The last thing he felt was his body changing form.

"Breathe."

Two facts struck Aleric; the woman's voice wasn't Lilian's and he couldn't suck in a breath. His lungs felt as though a dragon was standing on his chest. That had only happened once before, and it wasn't a pleasant experience.

"Come on," the woman urged. "Don't give up on me." She put her hand on his bare chest. The touch of her skin was cold. "Breathe," she repeated.

It took every ounce of strength Aleric could muster to pull a breath in. He held it for a moment, afraid it would be his last.

"Good," she said. There was a lilt to her voice that Aleric recognized but couldn't place. "I gave you the antidote for the gorgon bites. The paralysis will fade soon. Just keep breathing."

As sensation returned to his body, Aleric realized water was splashing on his face. He opened his eyes to see rain pouring down from a pitch black sky. It pounded on his bare chest. He tipped his head to see a pale face looking down at him. A slight, wry smile touched her lips.

Aleric's breath caught at the sight of the woman's pointed teeth.

"Calm down," she said. "You're going to undo everything I've accomplished." She shook her head. "You'd think a werewolf who just took on five gorgons and managed to wipe out three of them by himself would be a little steadier in the constitution department."

Aleric wanted to point out that it wasn't every day he awoke with his head on the lap of an eerily beautiful vampiress.

Her head jerked up.

"Your human is coming. I've got to go." She stood gracefully, easing his head to rest on the wet grass as she did so.

Aleric tipped his head to see her pick up a cloak from one of the gorgons. She spread it over his naked body.

"You can thank me for that later," she said. She looked in the opposite direction and trouble filled her gaze. "Promise me one thing, Aleric. Don't tell anyone about me."

He tried to speak, but the paralysis still gripped his throat. The fact that she knew his name sent a shiver across his skin.

"I'll take that as a yes," she said. She leaned down and touched his cheek. The gesture surprised him with its familiarity and gentleness. "Find me, Aleric."

"Aleric?" Lilian shouted.

Aleric looked in the direction of her voice. When he tipped his head back, the vampiress was gone.

"Aleric!" Lilian cried out.

He heard her run across the clearing. Lilian fell to her knees next to him. His clothes were clutched in her hand.

"Aleric, are you alright?" she asked. There was fear in her voice. "You killed them all!"

He followed her gaze to the gorgons. The one he had killed lay with its neck in an awkward position. The other two had fang marks in their throats. Blood colored the rain that pooled around the bodies.

Strength was returning far faster than Aleric had thought it would. He could breathe easier and the paralysis was fading, which made the ache in his shoulder return with a vengeance. Apparently being nearly squeezed to death by the massive coils of a gorgon wasn't doctor recommended. He made a mental note not to tell Nurse Eastwick about it.

Aleric pushed up and Lilian helped him to a sitting position.

"I can't believe you did that," she said.

"Did what?" Aleric asked.

Lilian gave him a straight look. "You took off so they

would follow you. They could've killed you."

Aleric knew just exactly how true that statement was. The vampiress' words echoed in his head. 'Don't tell anyone about me. Find me, Aleric.'

She had known his name. Perhaps she was hunting him like the gorgons had been. Maybe her presence there wasn't a coincidence at all. He felt strongly that was the case. But vampires and werewolves hated each other. Why would she risk her life to save his?

"Aleric?" Lilian repeated.

Aleric met her gaze. "Uh, sorry. I guess I'm a little shook up."

"I've never seen anything so terrifying," Lilian told him.

A thought occurred to Aleric. "Yet you tried to fight them with a tree branch."

The statement brought a small smile to Lilian's lips. "I suppose. I wasn't doing a very good job, though."

"You didn't get bit," Aleric replied. "So you did an excellent job. Trust me. You don't want to get bit by a gorgon."

"Did you get bit?" she asked.

Aleric heard the worry in her voice. He glanced down at his bare chest, but the bites were on his back and shoulders. He could still feel the lingering pain from the fang marks. At least she couldn't see them. He didn't want to concern her after what they had gone through.

"I'm fine," he told Lilian. "I just need a minute. Do you mind if I...." He indicated the clothes she held in her hand.

A slight blush touched Lilian's cheeks. She handed them to him and backed up. "Oh, not at all. I'll just wait in the trees back there, unless...." Her voice trailed away.

Aleric realized how much courage it had taken for her to run through the trees to find him. It was dark, pouring rain, and even the cellphone she held in a shaking hand didn't penetrate the blanket of night further than a foot. If there were more gorgons out there, he didn't want her running into them.

"Stay here," he said. He rose gingerly to his feet. His strength chose that embarrassing moment, with the gorgon's cloak clutched around his waist, to give out on him.

"Aleric!" Lilian exclaimed.

She caught his arm and leaned against him, helping him stand again. For a moment they stood there, her cheek against his bare chest and her arms around his middle. Warmth ran from wherever her skin touched and through Aleric's body. The scent of her hair, complete with the peach aroma of her shampoo, filled Aleric's nose. A tremble ran along his limbs. Aleric closed his eyes.

"Your heart is racing," she said quietly.

"Surviving does that to a person," Aleric replied. It sounded better than admitting that despite the fierce battle he had just fought, she was the one who made his heart beat so quickly.

He opened his eyes and looked down at her.

She lifted her gaze to him, her blue eyes bright and black hair soaked and dripping down her shoulders. He lifted a hand before he knew what he was doing, and he touched her cheek. He wanted to kiss her so badly in that moment that it was almost painful to deny the urge.

"We'd better get back to the car," Lilian whispered.

Aleric nodded and took a step back.

"Are you okay?" she asked.

"I'm fine," Aleric replied, his words barely audible above the pouring rain.

Lilian watched him for a moment, her gaze searching, before she turned around to give him his privacy.

Aleric pulled on his clothes, a task made difficult by his shoulder and all the more impossible because they were soaking wet. He debated whether it would be easier just to wear the gorgon's cloak, but it stunk like snake and he figured Lilian would probably be more comfortable if he wasn't wearing a skirt fashioned out of some killer Dark fae's only item of clothing.

He studied her frame as he finally worked his injured arm through the sleeve of his scrubs top and slipped it over his head. She was slender but not too skinny, her build one of health and activity. The way the rain made her beige shirt and dark blue jeans cling to her skin unsettled him. He ducked under the strap of the sling and managed to get his arm back in without too much jolting to the swollen joint, though by that point, any jolting was considerably too much.

"Shall we continue our walk?" he asked.

The look of uncertainty on Lilian's face when she turned back around gripped Aleric.

"What if the Second Horseman sent them?"

Aleric shook his head. "Fabian isn't one to meddle in the dark arts. Only those who truly understand the nature of such things can command the loyalty of a gorgon."

"Then who sent them?"

"That's what bothers me," Aleric told her honestly. "I have no idea why gorgons would be in Edge City, or outside of it like we are. They must be looking for something." He didn't say that the something they were looking for was a dashingly handsome but hopeless werewolf whose heart had been taken by one who had no idea of her power over him.

Aleric led the way to the path in silence. Lilian's small light from her phone flashed behind him. He heard her stumble, right herself, and stumble again. The want to hold her hand and guide her whispered in his mind, but he was afraid to be near her. His thoughts definitely weren't sound in her presence and if either of them had a chance of surviving the night, it would require his full attention to the matter at hand. He never should have brought her, and now she was entwined in the tapestry of mystery that had entangled Aleric since he had awaken to find himself in Edge City Hospital.

"That must be it," Lilian said.

Aleric's head jerked up. Yet again, the thought of Lilian had driven away the reality of danger or the task at hand. Aleric gave himself a mental kick. If he didn't learn how to keep his thoughts focused and away from her, neither of them would be safe.

"That looks like it," Aleric replied.

He led the way toward the small shack. The light from within its glowing windows turned the rain into drops of gold that vanished when they completed their fall past the panes. Aleric's senses thrummed with each step he took. He expected gorgons or worse to jump out at them, the creatures' presence hidden within the storm. If the gorgons had been waiting for them to find the Second Horseman, perhaps others were there as well. It would be the perfect opportunity to take Aleric unawares.

As if Lilian thought the same thing, her hand slipped into his.

Heat ran up Aleric's arm. He was tempted to let go and gain some space, but he couldn't will his fingers to open. They clung stubbornly and protectively to Lilian's smaller hand as if they had a mind of their own. Aleric cursed them mentally, but the other side of him rejoiced at how close she was, the way her jasmine and sunshine scent still lingered despite the way the rain tried so hard to banish it, and the sensation of her fingers fitting perfectly in his as if they were meant to be there.

"I'm pathetic," Aleric muttered.

"What was that?" Lilian asked.

Under her searching gaze, Aleric shook his head. "Uh, nothing. Just, well, nothing."

He let go of her hand under the pretense of needing to knock on the door. It actually wasn't an excuse; he supposed he could have knocked with his injured arm, but the pain would have made such an action ridiculous. In any case, he felt the excuse was a good one and stuck to it. After the knock, he attempted to cross his arms casually, but the sling made it difficult. Trying to cross them above, then below, and utterly failing, Aleric let his good arm drop and forced what he hoped was a calm smile but no doubt came across as psychotic. If she attempted to hold his hand again, he figured the best resolution would be to run off screaming into the trees. At least it would let her know how she made him feel.

"Come in." The words were followed by a sob.

Aleric and Lilian exchanged a glance.

"Is he crying?" Lilian whispered.

Aleric nodded. "Him or someone else."

He tried the door. The doorknob was unlocked. Aleric turned it and pushed the door inward. It swung with a loud creak that set his senses on edge.

"Why do doors like to do that?" Aleric asked.

"Doors are drama queens," Lilian replied, her voice light with only the barest hint of tremble to show how nervous she was to meet the Second Horseman.

"You're probably right," Aleric said with a nod. He led the way down the short hallway and kept up the banter to help Lilian relax. "I suppose if I hung there all day and night with only a few seconds of glory to spend whenever I opened and closed, I would definitely take advantage of it."

That brought a small laugh from Lilian. "Me, too," she

agreed.

Another sob made them both fall silent. Aleric listened and tested the air carefully for any indication that anyone other than Fabian was in the house. All signs pointed to the fact that the Second Horseman had been alone there for quite a while.

Aleric and Lilian peeked into the room. An extremely rotund man sat near the crackling fireplace, his head in his beefy hands and his rolls of fat quivering with each sob. On a small end table at his side sat a pair of weighing scales that appeared to be made of gold.

"That's the Second Horseman Famine?" Lilian asked in a whisper.

Aleric nodded. "He gets bigger whenever he takes nutrition from others. He's obviously been busy."

Just in case, Aleric whispered, "Wait here." He didn't know what state Fabian would be in, and he didn't want Lilian walking into harm's way.

Lilian nodded and stayed by the doorway. Aleric continued into the room.

"Uh, Fabian?"

The huge Horseman raised his head. Tears streamed down his face and into his thick black beard. His tiny eyes focused on Aleric. The big man's eyes widened and he lunged to his feet. Aleric backed up at the surprisingly fast movement from such a large person. He held up his hands, prepared to fight if need be.

Chapter Seven

"Aleric! Thank goodness you're here," Fabian said with a sob.

The huge Horseman wrapped Aleric in a tight hug. Aleric bit back an exclamation at the pain that coursed down his arm. He met Lilian's amused expression over the Horseman's shoulder. She gave him a small shrug as if to say she didn't know how to help. Aleric appreciated how hard she tried.

"Maybe you can help me," the Horseman said, still hugging Aleric. "I pray that you can. I'm so sad without him."

Aleric managed to work his way out of the Horseman's

bountiful grasp. He straightened his shirt and then his sling.

"How can I help, Fabian? You look horrible."

The big man nodded and collapsed back into the chair with another heart-wrenching sob. The chair gave a creak of protest. Fabian buried his face in his hands and his words came out muffled. "I know. I know. I just don't know what to do."

"So you chose to poison the tomatoes and run your brother's business into the ground?"

Fabian stared at up at the werewolf. "I didn't have a choice." Huge tears filled his eyes again. "I had to do it."

"Why?" Aleric asked. "You spread the plague to dozens of people. If we hadn't stopped Perry, the plague would be all over Edge City within the week."

"I know," Fabian replied. He gave a sweep of the arm to indicate himself, his expression one of disdain. "Look at me. Do you think I enjoy looking like this?" He sat back in his chair with a deep sigh. "I deserve to wallow in the consequences of my own actions. It's not like they've made a difference anyway, only broken Perry's heart and Fluffy still hasn't been returned."

That caught Aleric's attention. "Fluffy hasn't been returned? Was he supposed to be?"

"Who's Fluffy?" Lilian asked from the door.

Fabian's gaze swept past Aleric to the human. He quickly dabbed at his face with a corner of his shirt.

"I-I'm so sorry you have to see me like this," he apologized. He attempted to straighten his very damp shirt. "A woman shouldn't have to see a strong man this way, even if it does prove that he's sensitive and caring." His voice broke on the last word. "And I care about Fluffy so much!" Another sob took over and his buried his face in his hands again.

"Fluffy is Fabian's horse," Aleric explained.

"Perry's horse is named Buffy and Fabian's is Fluffy?" Lilian repeated.

The Horseman nodded. His watery gaze met hers. "Doyle's horse is named Duffy, and Wallace's is Bob."

"Bob?" Lilian repeated.

Fabian lifted a shoulder. "Wallace likes to create conflict. As the Horseman of War, it's his forte. We couldn't get him to go along with the other names, so Bob it is, Bob the big, blood red, intimidating and scary stallion." He gave Lilian a kind smile. "I secretly call him Muffy when Wallace isn't around. He'd be so mad if he knew."

"I'll keep your secret," Lilian promised.

Fabian gave another shuddering sigh. "But it doesn't matter because Fluffy's gone." His thick eyebrows pulled together as he spoke, willing Lilian to understand. "Fluffy's my best friend. He's more of a brother to me than those other Horsemen. At least he loves me and he doesn't force me to stay in this disgusting little hut poisoning tomatoes. I don't want to hurt Perry. I really do want him to be happy, but I'd do anything to get Fluffy back."

"What makes you think poisoning the tomatoes will bring Fluffy back?" Aleric asked.

Fabian waved toward the end table. Beneath the golden scales was a paper. Lilian pulled it free.

"Destroy the First Horseman's business or you'll never see Fluffy again," she read aloud.

"That's to the point," Aleric said. Lilian held out the paper. He took it and studied it. "So you poisoned the tomatoes and there's still no sign of Fluffy."

"That's right," Fabian replied. "It's got to be Wallace. He loves this kind of conflict. I'm sure he's laughing up a storm somewhere, enjoying how miserable he's made us both." The

Horseman's voice quivered. It looked like he was about to start sobbing again.

Aleric set a hand on the Horseman's shoulder. "Fabian, I will find Fluffy. You have my word. But you have to stop endangering lives. Don't poison the tomatoes. Let Perry's business flourish. He's happy here and I think he could actually make a good citizen of Edge City."

"You do?" Lilian and Fabian said at the same time.

Aleric nodded. "I do. I think it's about time this city accepts that differences can be good. Abnormalities can be strengths, and if Perry has a dream to own his own restaurant and feed people, he should be able to do so to his heart's content and not worry about endangering anyone's life."

A contented sigh escaped the Second Horseman. "That's beautiful, Aleric."

He moved as if to stand up again, but Aleric held out a hand. "No need to get up. Hugs aren't necessary; trust me." He honestly didn't think he could handle it again. "I'll find Wallace and get to the bottom of this."

"And I'll leave the tomatoes alone," Fabian promised. He gave Aleric a closer look. "Are you sure you haven't been eating Perry's pasta? You look nearly as bad as I feel."

Aleric gave him a dry smile. "I appreciate that, but I'm fine. We've got to get moving. In fact," he looked out the window as the thought occurred to him, "I know two little grims sleeping out in this weather. We need to get a tent to them right away."

"I love grims," Fabian replied. "Hold on a second."

He lumbered to his feet and made his way across the small shack. Aleric and Lilian exchanged a curious look at the man's sudden haste.

Fabian returned with two huge quilts in his arms. "These came with me from Blays. They'll keep those two little ones warm. You tell them that if they need a place to stay, old Fabian would be happy to take them in."

Lilian accepted the blankets.

Touched by the Horseman's generosity, Aleric nodded at him. "I'll let them know. I'd like to get them out of the streets, but they're a bit stubborn."

"Grims tend to be," Fabian replied. "When your whole life revolves around telling others when they're going to die, you get a bit stalwart in your attitude about the little things. I'd like to meet them."

"I'll mention it to them," Aleric promised.

He and Lilian walked back into the rain.

"That was unexpected," Lilian said.

"Fabian's got a soft heart. I knew he wouldn't poison people on purpose," Aleric replied. "I just wish I knew where to find Wallace."

"We'll find him," Lilian reassured him.

Aleric glanced at her through the rain. "Why do you sound so sure?"

She smiled at him. "Because you seem to be really good at making things work out."

That brought an answering smile to Aleric's face. "Thank you."

They drove to Dr. Worthen's house and Lilian brought out their tent. She also gathered a few other things that surprised Aleric, but he knew better than to argue. By the time they made it to the alley, it had been pouring for a few hours and Aleric was worried about how what state Grimma and Grimsli would be in.

"Grimma?" he called when Lilian pulled up to the curb. "Grimsli?"

The rain pounded around him; the huge drops hit the pavement so hard they splashed back up, soaking Aleric's legs as much as the rest of him. He held the tent awkwardly under one arm.

"Grimsli?" he repeated at the mouth of the alley.

"That's Dr. Wolf," he heard Grimma say to her brother.

"We're in here!" Grimsli called back.

Lilian reached Aleric's side with Fabian's quilts held in her arms. She didn't look thrilled about entering the dark alley, but Aleric was grateful when she followed closely behind him.

Aleric ducked at the entrance of the soaked cardboard.

"We brought you a tent. We thought…." Aleric's voice died away at what he saw.

The grim twins sat perfectly dry on the blankets Aleric had brought them before. They had a ragged picture book on their laps and gave Aleric matching smiles. Aleric stared at the cozy, dry cave they had made for themselves. Grocery bags had been stacked between the boxes, creating a runoff for the water. Two lanterns that look a little worse for the wear glowed near the middle of the floor. The grims' other possessions had been wrapped in more bags to keep dry. The pattering sound of drops on the roof was soothing.

"This is amazing," Lilian exclaimed when she crouched beside Dr. Wolf. "You don't even need a tent!"

"A tent?" Grimsli said.

"Tents are awesome!" Grimma replied.

Though Aleric had never set up a tent before, he attempted to help Lilian, Grimma, and Grimsli put together the one Lilian had brought. Grimsli had asked if they could set it up behind their cardboard cave so that nobody would see it from the street. Going along with the idea, Lilian was swift to shove the poles in the tracks and slip them into place.

"Maybe you should wait in the cave, Dr. Wolf," Grimma suggested the third time Aleric's tent pole refused to stay together long enough to be placed in the appropriate holes.

"It's just a little difficult," Aleric replied. The pole slipped again and he grabbed it with his left hand out of instinct. The answering pain made spots dance in his vision. "Perhaps you're right."

Aleric sat inside the little dome and watched Lilian and the twins. A few minutes later, Lilian had the tent up and the grims were happily sitting inside it planning how to expand their already cluttered little hut.

Lilian ducked back inside to join Aleric.

"They're cute, you know," she said.

Aleric nodded. "They're strong, considering what they've been through. You have to be strong out there."

"Blays doesn't sound like a very good place to live," Lilian noted.

Aleric motioned toward the mouth of the alley. "It's a lot like this, actually. The similarities surprise me sometimes." He paused, then said, "As do the differences."

"Like what?" Lilian asked.

Aleric eased back against the alley wall. The cardboard and grocery bags covering it kept him from getting wet.

"Well, in Blays, everyone is proud of what they do. They put their marks on everything. The sand wisps mark the glass with their handprints. The ironwork trolls never let anything leave their forges without their clan stamp, and you never see a lantern like that without the sparks wings' design on the bulb that shows itself wherever the light shines. It was the first thing that clued me in to the fact that I wasn't in Drake City when I awoke."

"I never heard that story," Lilian said. "How did you find yourself here?"

"I was running, then I was falling. I woke up at the hospital," Aleric replied. He could see it in his mind. The rain falling around him in a storm much like the one battering

Edge City, the pounding of his feet against the pavement, the sound of pursuit behind him. They would find him and he would pay. He had no doubt about that. Even the dark arts couldn't save him from the things he had done. He would have to pay.

"What is that?" Lilian asked.

Her words drew Aleric back to the present, to Edge City and the little alley they sat in. "What?" he asked.

"That look on your face," Lilian replied. She watched him closely; there was compassion in the depths of her eyes. "I've never seen anyone so sad."

Aleric forced a small smile. It was difficult. "Nothing," he lied. "Just a memory. Some things are better left forgotten."

She nodded, but he could see in her expression that she wanted to ask more questions, to find out about his past, to learn the things he didn't want to talk about.

"We'd better get back to the hospital," he suggested, rising. "I have patients to check on."

Lilian nodded. She ducked out of the small cardboard hut after him. "Dad will be worried, I'm sure. He likes me to check in with him, even though I am an adult."

The hint of frustration in her tone brought a smile to Aleric's face. "It's good that he cares so much. You should cherish that."

"I do," Lilian replied. She unlocked the car door. "It's just that sometimes I think worrying about me will send him to an early grave."

Aleric shook his head. "If the Fae Rift hasn't done it, I don't think anything will.

Lilian left him in the D Wing and went off to find Dr. Worthen. Aleric peeked into the Dark fae side and was relieved to see it empty. The sulfur scent of the plague victims lingered heavily in the air, but the poles on the far side of the room contained empty I.V. bags and there wasn't a patient to be seen. Aleric hoped that meant they had been able to go home.

He stepped into the Light fae side and paused at the sight of the sphinx watching him from beside the far window. A thrill of adrenaline made the fine hairs stand up on the back of Aleric's neck.

At the sight of him, the little black minky who had been sitting on the windowsill next to the sphinx let out a loud meow. She opened her wings and soared to the floor, then proceeded to gallop to Aleric, climb up his pant leg, sling, and shirt to sit on his shoulder, all the while meowing in protest about being left behind.

Aleric ran a finger over her soft head while keeping an eye on the sphinx.

"I didn't think you'd be up," he said.

The sphinx regarded him carefully. "Being tranquilized by a vampire isn't exactly something I planned for."

Aleric shook his head. "None of this is something we planned for. It just happened. We're trying to make the best of it."

The sphinx crossed his velvet paws in a humanlike gesture that belied the sharp claws within. "Is that what you expect me to do?"

"Yes," Aleric replied shortly.

The sphinx's eyes narrowed. "Why?"

Aleric held his gaze. "Because wreaking havoc on an all-human society that is still coming to terms with the fact that the fae exist wouldn't be polite."

The sphinx gave a quiet snort. "Politeness isn't my forte."

"Yeah, well dealing with cats isn't mine," Aleric replied. As if in answer, Diablo rubbed her head against Aleric's chin. He assisted her down to her favorite spot in his sling and smoothed her black-feathered wings with gentle fingers.

"She seems to think otherwise."

Aleric kept his voice level and his gaze on the kitten when he replied, "Well, minkies aren't prone to prejudice."

"Is that what you think this is?" the sphinx asked with surprise in his voice.

Aleric looked up at him. "You yelled 'Revenant' and attacked my friend."

The sphinx's claws slid out of his paws even though he kept his arms crossed in a façade of calm. "I'll never trust anyone who trusts a vampire."

"That's prejudice," Aleric replied calmly. He could feel the tension rising in the room. As much as his normal instincts were to goad the sphinx into fighting, he had to remind himself what was on the line. "Look," Aleric said. "I'm sorry. We didn't get off on the right foot, and I'm not making it any better. Old habits die hard."

The werewolf crossed the room toward the sphinx. The Light fae creature watched him with a narrow gaze. "The Rift has thrown everyone here into a different environment than we're used to on Blays. Here, it's not werewolf against vampire, Light fae against Dark. It can still be, but the way I see it, changes have to be made for our survival." He paused a few feet from the sphinx and set the minky on the next windowsill. The kitten rubbed her head against his hand.

"Changes like trusting a vampire?" the sphinx said in a doubtful tone.

"Yes," Aleric replied. When the sphinx opened his mouth to argue, Aleric held up a hand. "I know. Believe me. I didn't trust him when he first got here, either. But since then, Dartan and I have saved each other's lives multiple times and he has turned out to be a very level-headed friend." At the sphinx's sound of disbelief, Aleric gave him a straight look. "I know. If my old pack ever knew, they wouldn't speak to me again. But you know what?"

He waited until the sphinx finally said, "What?"

"My pack is dead," Aleric replied, his tone cold. "They were killed by vampires and demons, both races of which I've been forced to work with since I have been here. It hasn't been easy, but I've done my best because this situation is bigger than me and it's bigger than you. I've had to deal with some pretty tough decisions here that in Blays I never would have faced. I could've gone back."

He saw the sphinx's gaze lighten with interest and the werewolf nodded. "And I'll help you get back home, but I'm staying here because I'm sick and tired of living in a world where every action I made was viewed with suspicion and every dream I ever had was pounded into the dust because Ashstock aren't worth a dragon's gizzard stone in Blays." He held the sphinx's gaze. "All I ask is that while you're here, you have the decency to give those I work with a little respect because they've gone far above and beyond to save the lives of fae like us without asking for anything in return."

The sphinx kept quiet. Aleric thought he would argue or attack, but the sphinx's claws slid slowly back into his paws. He nodded. "Fine. I'll keep the peace."

"That's all I ask," Aleric replied.

He gave the minky one last pat and left with the thought that at least the two cats could keep each other company, though he felt bad for abandoning Diablo with such a dour companion.

Aleric pushed through the doors to the Emergency Room and found Nurse Eastwick in Dr. Worthen's office with the doctor and Lilian.

"Sounds like you've been busy," Dr. Worthen noted.

Aleric could tell by his tone that the doctor wasn't thrilled about his inclusion of Lilian in his travels, but wouldn't say so in front of his daughter. Aleric felt a rush of gratitude for Lilian's presence because he wasn't in the mood for a lecture on reckless endangerment after his argument with the sphinx.

"I noticed that the plague victims are out of the D Wing. How are they recovering?" he asked the doctor.

"Much better," Dr. Worthen replied. "They're responding to the I.V.s and their symptoms are abating much faster than we anticipated. We've sent quite a few home, though we've had several strange incidents."

That caught Aleric's attention. "What kind of incidents?"

Dr. Worthen sat back in his chair. "A few have mentioned hallucinating about death and dying. I feel it's a side-effect of the plague and have them meeting with our psychiatrist for mandatory evaluations before they're released so we're sure they are fit to return to their families."

"Good call," Aleric agreed. "How's the elf doing?"

"That's what I came here about," Nurse Eastwick replied. She looked from Dr. Worthen to Aleric. "I need your opinions. Dartan's waiting for us."

The nurse refused to expound as the doctors followed her down the hallway. Lilian fell in beside Aleric. At his questioning gaze, she lifted a shoulder. "I'm bored."

"You should be resting," Dr. Worthen replied, looking back at her. "You'd be doing much better if you weren't off gallivanting with Dr. Wolf all around the city."

Aleric gave the doctor an apologetic look. "I needed a ride. Ask Gregory. I shouldn't be allowed behind the wheel of any vehicle in this city if you don't want more patients in your Emergency Room."

The orderly stuck his head out of one of the partitioned rooms they passed. "That's for sure."

"Thanks," Aleric said dryly.

"Any time," the orderly replied.

"So you were merely chauffeuring?" Dr. Worthen said. "I suppose that's not so bad. But I would appreciate it if you would take it easy."

"I will," Lilian promised. She gave Aleric a wide-eyed look of relief.

Aleric fought back a smile and followed the others into the room.

Dr. Worthen picked up the file near the patient's bed. He thumbed through it with a concerned expression.

"Hey, Wolfie," Dartan said with a nod from his seat near the bed. "Good work with Perry. Lilian told me about your meeting with him to stop the spread of the plague."

"I thought you were just the driver," Dr. Worthen said, spearing his daughter with an accusatory look.

"Uh, well, this is about the elf," Lilian replied. "How's she doing, Loreen? She looks really pale."

"Her vitals are still dropping," Nurse Eastwick answered. "We're fearing an infection or worse from whatever it was that attacked her."

Aleric's instincts thrummed. "You said worse," Aleric replied. "What do you mean?"

"We found some strange marks," Nurse Eastwick continued. She pulled down the edge of the elf's gown to show two little marks on one clavicle. She showed similar marks on the elf's arm and again on her ankle. "What do you think these could be?"

A knot tightened in Aleric's stomach with each reveal.

"Here," he said quietly. "Look." With Lilian's help, he slipped his arm out of the sling and pulled his shirt off over his head. He turned around to show them his back. "Are they the same distance apart as these?"

The surprised silence that filled the room was broken by

the quiet beeping of the monitor near the elf's head.

"Yes, they are," Nurse Eastwick said. "Aleric, what are those?"

Aleric pulled the shirt back on and faced them again. He kept his gaze on his sling, pretending to struggle with the strap so that he didn't have to face what he knew was coming.

"Gorgon bites."

"Gorgon bites!" Dartan repeated. He stood from his chair. "How on Blays did you get bit by gorgons?"

"You got bit?" Lilian said with horror in her voice.

"You know what gorgons are?" Dr. Worthen demanded of his daughter.

Aleric let out a breath and lifted his head. "I need to talk with Dartan for a minute in private."

Dr. Worthen shook his head. "I need answers. You can't keep secrets if this elf's life depends on it. I know the things you've gotten into might not be pretty." He glanced at Lilian and his gaze narrowed. "But you've dragged my daughter into it and endangered yourself. I need to know what's going on."

Aleric shook his head. "I don't know exactly what I've gotten myself into and I need a sounding board before I spread unnecessary panic." He put a hand on the doctor's shoulder. "I need you to trust me. Have I given you any reason not to?"

He waited until Dr. Worthen gave a reluctant shake of his head. "No, you haven't."

Aleric dropped his hand. "I've nearly died to protect this hospital. Give me the benefit of the doubt that if something I learn will save a life, I'll do it. That's all I ask."

It took a moment, but Dr. Worthen finally nodded. "You deserve at least that. I'm sorry."

Aleric gave him an understanding look. "It's been a crazy

day and night for me, and I can't imagine how it's been for all of you dealing with the plague victims. I just need a few minutes to get my thoughts in order so I know the next step we need to take."

"I'd recommend Minnow's," Dr. Worthen said with acceptance in his voice. "Just promise me you'll come talk when you have things figured out."

"I will," Aleric replied.

Chapter Eight

"At least try the pie," Aleric said. "It's not going to kill you."

"It might," Dartan replied. He eyed the chocolate and whipped cream-covered wedge in front of him. "It's the wrong color."

Aleric rolled his eyes. "Everything good doesn't come in red," he said.

"That's where you're wrong," Dartan pointed out. He poked the pie suspiciously with his fork. "Blood is red. Blood is good. Blood is all I eat and all I need. Therefore, in my opinion, everything good comes in red."

"Vampires," Aleric said with a shake of his head.

A sound caught his ear. Aleric turned and caught Iris' hand before the waitress could plunge her knife into Dartan's chest. Dartan watched with mild amusement as the werewolf spun out of his seat, twisting the waitress' arm so that she dropped the knife. It fell to the table with a clatter.

Aleric stood behind Iris still holding her wrist in his good arm. His chest heaved.

"What are you doing?" he demanded.

"S-saving your life," Iris replied.

Aleric let go of her hand. "How?"

She stepped back to face him while keeping Dartan in view at all times.

"I heard him say he was a v-vampire," she pointed out, her voice shaking. "I thought he would hurt you."

"Dartan's my friend," Aleric told her. "I wouldn't have brought him here if he wasn't."

She shook her head, her gaze never leaving Dartan's amused one. "What if he was controlling you? I've heard stories."

Aleric gave her a small smile. "There are lots of stories about vampires out there." He looked at Dartan. "Some of the fear is well-founded, but Dartan is a vampire with perfectly good manners, even though he refuses to try Minnow's famous mud pie." He lowered his voice. "Although we mustn't hold that against him. Vampires are known for their extremely bland palettes."

"I heard that," Dartan said.

"Are you sure you're alright?" Iris asked as Aleric sat back in his seat.

"I'm fine and perfectly safe," Aleric replied. "But I appreciate your concern." He paused, and when Iris appeared reluctant to leave despite his reassurances, he asked, "Would it be greedy of me to request two grilled cheese sandwiches? I know two children who would be so grateful for them."

Iris looked from Aleric to Dartan and back again. She finally nodded. "Not at all," she told him. "I'll get those for you right away."

"There's no rush," Aleric replied. "I'm sure they'd prefer them warm."

"I'll have them ready when you leave," Iris told him. She walked away with only one backwards glance to show her confusion about what had just happened.

"Bland palettes?" Dartan repeated. "I have a very exacting palette, if I do say so myself. I prefer my blood to be O Positive because it contains just a hint of—"

Aleric shook his head with a sigh. "I really can't take you anywhere, can I?"

Dartan replied dryly, "Wolfie, you took a vampire to a diner. What am I supposed to do, supply my own beverage?"

"I happen to know for a fact that you ate before we headed over here, and if you could stop referring to yourself as a vampire, it might make both of our lives a bit easier," Aleric replied.

He looked around to see if any of the other diners were alarmed by their conversation, but the couple in far booth and the three young men at the table in the middle of the diner appeared not to notice them.

"It is cute how she rushed to your rescue," Dartan noted. "Perhaps you have some charm after all."

Aleric felt his cheeks heat up. "That was nothing. I met Iris the other day when I was in here and she was kind enough to give me a massage...."

Dartan's eyebrows rose with interest. "A massage! Well. You do get around, Wolfie Boy. I'm proud of you."

Aleric rolled his eyes. "Her sister is a masseuse and she saw me rubbing my shoulder. She massaged it for a few minutes before my food was ready. It was nothing."

"Nothing," Dartan replied, his tone indicating that it was anything but. "I saw a twinkle in her eyes. Is there love there, one is left to wonder?"

Aleric sat back in the booth with a shake of his head. "That's ridiculous."

Dartan leaned forward and put his elbows on the table. "I've never known a werewolf to call love ridiculous. Your race is, how shall I put it, extremely impulsive and stubborn on the subject of love."

Aleric thought of Lilian. He stared at his pie, his appetite replaced by emptiness. He wasn't going to voice the thoughts in his head, but the words spilled out anyway. "I see love as this elusive thing, heartbreaking, yet sweet. I long for it and fear it at the same time."

He felt Dartan's stare, but refused to look up.

"I didn't know werewolves were poets," the vampire finally said.

Aleric pushed his pie back and looked at the vampire. "We're not. At least, I'm not. And for all I know, I'm the last of us, so that doesn't leave much hope for the race."

Dartan gave him a closer look. "What's got you so morose all of the sudden?"

Aleric shook his head. "Now's not the time or place for this discussion. We were supposed to talk about gorgons, remember?"

Dartan sat back, his expression stubborn. "I remember, but I feel like this is important. I've never heard you talk this way. I take great pride in the fact that I am the best friend of the famous Doctor Wolf." He grinned when Aleric rolled his eyes and continued, "What kind of a bestie would I be if I missed the not-so-subtle clues that the said doctor is wallowing in a self-created pit of miserable despair?"

That brought a chuckle from Aleric. "It's not quite that bad."

Dartan lifted an eyebrow. "I just heard a werewolf say love is elusive and he fears it."

"You're taking my words out of context," Aleric began.

Dartan cut him off. "Am I? Really? Take one look at yourself in the mirror. On second thought, don't. The glass will probably shatter from the completely miserable sorrow of your expression right now. Seriously, Wolfie, you have a severe problem, and if that cute waitress and her obvious crush on you doesn't help it, I fear nothing will."

Aleric allowed a small smile to touch his lips. "She doesn't have a crush on me."

"She braved nearly slaying the big, bad vampire to save your life, didn't she?" Dartan asked.

Aleric nodded.

"People do crazy things in the name of love, Doc. Trust me. I know what I'm talking about."

Aleric stared at him. "You were in love?"

Dartan put a pale hand over his heart. "Are you insinuating by your skeptical tone that because a vampire doesn't have a fully functioning cardiovascular system the way werewolves do, that our hearts cannot bleed in agony at the mere thought of an unreturned gesture, that we cannot mourn the distance of an adored one's feelings, that we cannot pine away after love lost or sob our lonesome selves to dreamless sleep when such love is found unrequited?"

"That's a bit dramatic," Aleric pointed out.

Dartan gave a heartfelt sigh. "You live but the span of a human's years; can you not imagine the agony of a thousand such years spent in unreciprocated yearning, unanswered worship, and even unrequited total and helpless desire for the briefest lift of the lips that could hint at a smile?" He leaned back in the booth with another loud sigh. "Alas, the torment of a vampire's heart is misunderstood at best and disregarded at worst."

Aleric waited until the vampire stopped speaking to ask, "Are you being serious?"

Dartan sat back up. "I'm being dramatic. I thought you could tell the difference."

Aleric raised a hand to catch Iris' attention.

"What are you doing?" Dartan asked.

"I'm going to tell her to go ahead and stab you," Aleric replied.

"Alright, fine," Dartan said. "It's true. I was in love once."

By his tone, Aleric could tell the admission was a hard one. He watched his friend, hoping that silence would goad him forward the way questions never seemed to.

Dartan picked up his fork and toyed with the whipped cream on top of the pie. "That's not something I admit lightly," he said without taking his eyes from the fork.

White covered the tines. To Aleric's surprise, the vampire pushed his plate to the side and began drawing on the table with the edge of one tine.

"She was beautiful." Dartan's tone took on a wistful note. He dipped the fork back into the whipped cream and continued his drawing as he spoke. "Hers was the kind of beauty that made the songbirds still and the crickets fall silent in her wake for fear of breaking the harmony that followed her. She was special." Dartan looked up at Aleric for a brief moment. "She could talk to ghosts."

"Ghosts?" Aleric repeated, his voice quiet for fear of ending Dartan's openness.

"Ghosts," Dartan said again. A slight smile touched the corners of his mouth. "I don't know if she was thrilled about it, but she accepted it as a gift instead of the curse most would consider it to be."

He used more whipped cream, creating lines and circles Aleric couldn't interpret from his seat.

"The ghosts trusted her. Anyone would trust her," Dartan continued. "She had that special skill. She could walk into a room and immediately everyone was calm. There could be an entire brawl, but the moment she entered, it would stop as though everyone had an agreement that there would be no violence in her presence."

There was love in Dartan's words. It was undeniable. Aleric could see it in the intensity with which Dartan watched his whipped cream creation on the table, and in the way his free hand twitched whenever he mentioned her as though a part of him still longed to hold her hand.

"You were young," Aleric guessed, his words soft.

Dartan nodded. He was quiet for so long Aleric thought he was finished speaking. The werewolf was about to ask a question when Dartan took a shallow breath.

"We were young and I was foolish to think that my father would ever allow such an interest." He gripped the fork so tight the metal bent in an arch. Dartan blinked and looked down at the utensil. He gave a little sigh and dipped the tines in the whipped cream once more. "I met Rowe when I was sixteen. She was only fifteen."

Dartan smiled as if he couldn't help himself. It was an expression Aleric had never seen on the vampire's face before. His piercing red gaze softened, the lines on his forehead disappeared, and for a moment, just a moment, Aleric could imagine him as a sixteen-year-old vampire meeting the girl of his dreams for the first time.

"She had curly blonde hair that she tossed behind her shoulder with an impatient gesture as though she had no time for its silliness. She used to threaten to cut it all off, only because she knew I would reply that I would shave my head bald in protest. She loved my hair." Dartan gave a self-deprecating smile and pulled at a strand of his black hair. "The thought of me bald at sixteen would send her into fits of giggles. It was my favorite sound in all of Blays."

The happiness in the vampire's gaze changed to one of sorrow. His lips pressed into a flat line as he looked down at the sketch on the table.

"It's strange, isn't it?" he asked musingly. "The thing I loved about Rowe was that she made me feel more like a human and less like a beastly, blood-devouring vampire." He shook his head. "I would be the first to tell you that to deny your heritage is to deny your path." He looked up at Aleric. "And before you accuse me of poetry or oracle-like wit, let me note that it was my mother who told me such things." His voice lowered along with his gaze. "I suppose it was her way of helping me accept myself before her death."

"How did she die?" Aleric asked quietly.

"My father killed her," Dartan replied. "I guess now you'll understand why he was so upset I fell in love with a human at school."

Shock filled Aleric to the point that he couldn't speak. He heard a gasp behind him and glanced back to see Iris and another other waitress listening to the story. Dartan's gaze flickered to them and then back to the table as if he had known of their presence all along.

He had drawn a few more lines when Iris said, "Please continue."

"You can't leave us hanging," an older waitress who wrapped silverware in napkins with thin, worn hands, urged.

The woman's nametag said 'Dottie'.

Dartan sat back with a smile and a slightly detached expression that told Aleric he was done with baring his soul to the world. He gave a flourish with one hand and said, "Though her presence is but a memory to me, I will never forget the beauty of her face."

Both waitresses crossed to Dartan's side, all fear of the vampire forgotten. As soon as they turned to see what he had created, hands flew to their faces and looks of shock filled their expressions.

"I have never seen anything so lovely," Dottie exclaimed.

Iris nodded. "It's as if everything beautiful about a young woman is contained in this one face. No wonder you fell for her so hard."

Curious, Aleric rose and walked around to the other side of the table. He reached Dartan's side and his mouth dropped open.

The face could have been carved out of marble for all of its grace. Somehow, the vampire had managed to give such depth and expression to her eyes that it felt as though they stared into Aleric's soul. The curl of her hair around her forehead gave her a youthful appearance along with the slight lift of one eyebrow that hinted at a teasing, cheerful demeanor. The simple lines of her lips contained the whisper of a smile that made the viewer grin in return. The curve of her cheek and the tilt of her chin told of a happy character and youthful spontaneity as though she planned to change the world.

"She's an angel," Aleric said, his words just above a whisper.

Dartan's hand slid across the drawing, wiping it from view. Aleric jerked back at the simple action and saw the two waitresses do the same out of the corner of his eye. Loss filled him for a moment as if he had also known her, only to have her taken away. He had to remind himself that she had only been a drawing created with a fork and a helping of whipped cream.

"You have a rare talent," Dottie said.

Iris nodded. "I wish I had thought to take a picture of that," she said, her tone one of regret. "Nobody will believe me."

"If you tell them a vampire came into Minnow's and drew a young woman's face on the table with cream and a utensil, they'll have you hauled away for sure," Dartan replied with his easy smile.

Both of the waitresses smiled back. Aleric fought down the urge to roll his eyes. Leave it to Dartan to capture the heart of every woman within his reach.

"Can I get you anything else, love?" Dottie asked.

"Your smile is enough for me," Dartan replied.

A blush ran across the older woman's face. Iris giggled and grabbed Dottie's hand. They both hurried to the kitchen.

"Did you make that up?" Aleric accused. He couldn't deny the way the story and the drawing had moved him, but he also wasn't sure how far the vampire would go to woo the whims of the women around him.

Dartan shook his head. "If I did, it would have had a happy ending. Believe it or not, even I have a heart." He held up a hand before Aleric could say anything and concluded, "Even if it isn't in a fully functioning cardiovascular system, it does have the ability to feel pain." The vampire cleared his throat and picked up the napkin he had set on his lap despite the fact that he hadn't eaten a single bite. He proceeded to wipe the whipped cream off of his hand with slow, careful movements. "Now, back to your gorgon problem. We're here because you got bit."

While Aleric wanted to hear what had happened to the girl Dartan had loved, the elf's life depended on the vampire's assistance. His shoulder ached. He pull his arm carefully out of the sling and rested it on the table. The different angle helped ease the pain.

"There's a vampiress in the city."

Aleric doubted anything else he could have said would have had such an effect on the vampire.

Dartan's head lifted, his movements to wipe away the whipped cream from his hand forgotten. His fingers opened and the napkin drifted to the floor with the grace of an autumn leaf from a tree. The vampire stared at Aleric as if a goblin had crawled from his mouth or an anansi spider dangled in front of his face. For the first time since Aleric had met him, Dartan appeared actually and completely speechless.

"Did you hear me?" Aleric repeated. "I said—"

Dartan cut him off with a simple gesture of his hand. "There's a vampiress in the city."

The way the vampire repeated the words gave them a whole different meaning than Aleric's had contained. The tone of dread, the resounding horror, and the expression of sheer fear in the vampire's red eyes sent a chill down Aleric's spine.

"You don't need to repeat yourself," Dartan said in a voice that was barely a whisper. "The first time was bad enough."

"Bad enough?" Aleric echoed. "She saved my life."

Dartan shook his head. "You must be mistaken. Vampiresses never save lives. That's against their entire code. They drain the lives of others and throw them away, forgotten, abused, neglected, and alone."

Aleric cracked a smile. "Did you perhaps have a vampiress mistress…?"

"Don't!" Dartan said sharply, cutting him off again. There was no humor in the vampire's red eyes. He looked around as if worried she would appear behind him. He locked onto Aleric's gaze. "Don't you dare joke around about this. If you're making this up…."

Aleric shook his head at the accusation in the vampire's words. "I saw her with my own eyes."

Dartan let out a hiss through his teeth. "The city is doomed."

"She saved my life," Aleric said. "Did you hear me the first time? What is wrong with you? Aren't you overreacting? You look like you've seen a ghost and you just finished telling me a story of a girl you loved who spoke to ghosts, so you'd think you would be used to it."

Dartan's eyes narrowed. "Have you ever seen me look like this?" he demanded.

Aleric thought about it, then shook his head.

"When we faced the Archdemon and I nearly burned to death twice, did I look like this?"

Aleric shook his head again.

"When I pretended to turn you over to my father as a sacrifice only to defeat him using wood nymph blood and then send him back as a prisoner to Blays, did I look like this?"

Aleric didn't shake his head; he felt the action was unnecessary by that point.

Dartan leaned across the table toward him. "Aleric, if I look like this, it's because there's a reason. Before this one, have you ever met an actual vampiress?"

Aleric waited. When Dartan refused to continue until he answered the question, he sighed and shook his head. "No, I haven't."

Dartan sat back and crossed his arms in front of his chest.

"Then don't you ask if I'm overreacting. Have you ever thought about the fact that every vampire my father brought to Edge City was male?"

The thought caught Aleric by surprise. "I haven't."

Dartan let out a breath. "At the most, Blays has perhaps three Vampiresses at a time. Do you know why?" He didn't wait for Aleric to answer this time. "Because they kill each other off. Vampiresses are stronger than vampires, hungrier, and far more vicious. Think of my merciless, heartless father; even he chose a human woman to give him the heir he needed rather than face the wrath of a vampiress. Allow that a moment to settle in."

Aleric waited for a drop of condensation to reach the bottom of his glass of milk before he said, "She saved me from the gorgons. I took down three, but I was bitten. I would have died if she hadn't given me the antidote."

Understanding showed in Dartan's gaze. "So you're expecting she has another antidote on hand for the elf."

Aleric nodded. "It may be the only hope she has."

Dartan shook his head. "You're resting that elf's life on the good nature of a vampiress. We might as well plan her funeral."

"Dartan!" Aleric said. "I have to try."

When it was obvious the werewolf wasn't going to budge, Dartan gave in. "Tell me about your encounter with her."

Chapter Nine

"The only way to find a vampiress is to follow the carnage."

"You've said that before," Aleric told Dartan as he followed the vampire through another dark alley.

Edge City had plenty of deep, dusky, muck-layered alleys to traverse. Aleric checked the corners, layers, and heights with his senses straining until he was so tense he felt like he would explode. It didn't help that the vampire he followed kept making the same droll statements over and over.

"We haven't found any carnage," Lilian pointed out yet

again.

"We'll know it when we see it," Dartan repeated himself for the hundredth time. "It's hard to miss the lair of such a blood-thirsty fiend."

Aleric sighed. "You're going with 'fiend'," he repeated, his weariness showing in his tone. "You'd think after so many centuries of life, vampires would come up with a better vocabulary."

Dartan snorted as he stepped over a pile of refuse.

The squeaks of several rats sounded; Lilian went around the rubble instead. Aleric followed, his gaze on the pile in case a lacuda appeared. He knew the huge snakes were only in Blays, but habits wrought through hard-earned experience died just as hard.

"I could say she's an unforgiving mistress of consummate wretchedness and villainy," Dartan suggested.

Lilian gave him a sideways glance. "How about a soul-sucking wench filled with abhorrent and abysmal vileness?"

Dartan cracked a smile and elbowed Aleric. "I like her. She can stay."

"Where?" Aleric asked. "In this alley? Now you just sound creepy. I don't understand how so many women are attracted to you."

Lilian tripped over a bottle in the dark alley. Before Aleric could react, Dartan was there to catch her and right her with a vampire's grace.

"Centuries of practice," Dartan said with a wink at Lilian before he let go of her hand. "It's not really fair to you, Wolfie. You've a mere twentyish years when I've had lifetimes to perfect the art of wooing."

Lilian smirked. "I'll bet if you call it wooing to their faces, the women would laugh."

Aleric grinned.

Dartan gave her an appalled stare. "You dare mock me after I practically saved your life there?"

"I tripped," Lilian said dryly. "I think I would have survived."

"With your clothes stained by who knows what kind of rubbish fills these vacant streets," Dartan pointed out. "Are you saying my charms fail to impress someone as delicate and graceful as you?"

Lilian gave an unfeminine snort that endeared Aleric to her all the more. "I grew up mopping the hospital floors and cooking for Dad and me when I was six. I'm far from delicate. And as for graceful—"

Aleric was watching her closely, and this time when she tripped, he was ready to catch her arm before the vampire could so much as blink. The action caused a jolt through his shoulder, but he didn't let it show. The approving and surprised expression on Dartan's face was enough to make him grin, while the warmth in Lilian's eyes made the pain far worth it.

"You have your own kind of grace," Aleric told her. He made sure she was steady before he let go of her hand.

"Thank you," she replied with a touch of red to her cheeks.

Dartan's eyebrows rose. "You're smooth, for a werewolf."

Lilian laughed. "You sound surprised. I thought you were friends."

"We are," Aleric replied. "It's just that Dartan seems to take *wooing*, as he calls it, as a personal challenge to spite me."

Dartan opened his mouth in mock horror and put a pale hand to his chest. "It's not a challenge when one is as skilled at it as I."

"You'll have to step up your game if you want to impress

me," Lilian said. "I have a thing for brown-eyed, handsome werewolves."

She shot Aleric a teasing look and a thrill of warmth ran across his skin.

Dartan shook his head and led the way to the next alley. "If you think this werewolf is like any other of his race, you would be sorely mistaken. I fear he has corrupted your way of thinking about his Ashstock species. They're vile creatures, filled with fleas and ideas about pack above country and all that. I'm afraid he represents his race about as much as a faun represents the upper half of the caprid family."

Lilian glanced at Aleric. He shrugged his shoulders. "They're half-goat from only the waist-down, so I guess not well."

Dartan led the way into the next alley, still speaking over his shoulder. "Werewolves will never be fully human, no matter how hard they try to pretend not to want to sniff the closest lamp post or—"

"Stop!"

"Don't get testy, Wolfie," Dartan continued. "I'm just clarifying a few—"

Aleric grabbed Dartan's shoulder and pulled him roughly backwards. The scent was so strong in his nose he had to open his mouth to breathe. "Lacuda."

Dartan stared at him as if he had sprouted two heads. "They're a myth."

"What's a lacuda?" Lilian asked.

"They're not a myth," Aleric replied. "I've seen one in Drake City."

"Giant children-eating snakes?" Dartan argued. "They're what mothers use to get their children to come inside at night. I've always wondered what sort of woman has to threaten their children with nightmares. It's a story; a wives' tale."

"Speaking of tails," Aleric said quietly.

He pointed. Dartan and Lilian followed his finger. Dartan swore quietly under his breath.

The sight of the unmistakable black and gold pattern across the scales made Aleric's heart race. He moved Lilian behind him.

"The tail is wider around than I am," she said in a horrified whisper. "What do we do?"

"Get as far away from here as possible," Dartan replied, pushing past them.

Aleric grabbed the vampire's arm. "We can't leave it here."

"We very well can," Dartan said, jerking his arm free. "We can pretend we didn't see it the same way I saw a woman in front of the hospital let her dog leave its excrement on the sidewalk and then walk away as though she had no idea of what it had done. Nurse Eastwick wasn't thrilled when the said excrement covered the bottom of her shoe later. I would have warned her, but as you know, I have a severe allergy to the sun and didn't want to risk it over excrement."

Aleric had never heard the vampire babble before. He looked closer at his friend. Dartan's face was paler than usual, which was saying a lot considering he was a vampire. He drummed his fingers on his thigh in a quick outer fingers-inner fingers pattern. He kept glancing behind them as if making sure the snake hadn't moved to block their path to safety.

"You're afraid of snakes." Aleric said the statement in a flat tone.

"Terrified," Dartan replied immediately. "If only my father could see me now. He'd be so proud." He kept his gaze on the snake's tail when he said, "He used to hide his pet lacuda under my covers. To this day, I can't sleep with blankets."

"So you knew they existed," Aleric pointed out.

Dartan nodded. "His was not yet fully grown. Thank you for fulfilling the worst of my fears with the knowledge that they do indeed eat small children."

"It could probably eat large adults, given the size of the snake," Lilian said.

Dartan gave her a horrified look. "Are you some sort of devil or something? Why do you torment me?"

The tightness of Lilian's voice revealed her fear when she said, "I'm terrified as well, but I never thought I'd see a vampire reduced to a puddle at the sight of a few scales."

"A few?" Dartan sputtered. "A few?" He swung his pale hand around to point it accusingly at the snake's tail. "If that is any indication, we'd have enough skin to make a house, if that made any sense at all." He shook his head and grabbed both of their hands in an uncharacteristically forward manner. "Come on. I told myself the vampiress would be the death of me, now I find myself hoping so. Let's hunt her and forget about the coils of doom that lay beneath that rubbish."

Lilian allowed herself to be led away, but Aleric pulled his hand free. "What if someone else comes down this alley?"

Dartan's shoulders tensed. His footsteps slowed. He finally stopped near the street, but refused to look at Aleric.

"No one would know what to do," Aleric said. "It could stay here gorging on people and pets for years. Imagine how many lives would suffer because you walked away."

Aleric was terrified of the creature as well, but the sight of the vampire so filled with fear for some reason pushed him to be the strong one. He didn't know how to take care of the problem any more than they did, but he refused to allow one more person to suffer from the aftermath of the Rift if he could help it.

Silence filled the air. Lilian looked from Dartan to Aleric.

"I hate you," Dartan finally said.

"I know," Aleric replied. He smiled when the vampire came back with Lilian close behind.

"Wipe that smug grin off your face," Dartan demanded. He passed Aleric and paused at the same place as before. He crossed his arms in front of his chest. "So what do you propose we do?"

"I knew you'd do the right thing," Aleric said. "I think this city is making you soft."

Dartan shook his head, but didn't take his gaze off the snake.

"How do you handle one of those?" Lilian asked.

Aleric admired the brave front she put on. He could smell the fear wafting from her and Dartan even through the musk of snake, yet she kept calm and it was obvious her cool façade affected even the vampire.

"As carefully as possible," Aleric said. "The sooner we can get it back to Blays, the better."

Dartan stared at him. "You want to send it back?"

"Yes," Aleric replied, baffled. "What's your plan?"

"Chop it into tiny pieces and hope to Blays we don't find anyone inside its belly," Dartan said.

To Aleric's surprise, Lilian was nodding, too. "We can't send it back if it really does eat children in alleyways. That's just horrible. But we can't kill it, either."

"Yes, we can," Dartan cut in. "And by 'we', I mean 'Wolfie.'"

Lilian ignored him. "There has to be something else we can do."

Aleric thought for a moment. "Do you have a phone?"

"In my car," Lilian replied. "Why?"

"I think we should see if the Police Commissioner has any ideas," Aleric said.

Dartan nodded emphatically. "I agree. It's their city. We'll let them deal with it."

"We'll help them deal with it," Aleric said.

Lilian hurried back toward the vehicle.

"You know pretending to be the brave werewolf is pathetic," Dartan said.

Aleric glanced at him. "I'm as scared of the snake as you are."

"Right," Dartan said in a derisive tone.

Aleric grinned. "You're right. I'm not. Lilian nailed it when she said you turned into a puddle at the sight of it. I've never seen a vampire so scared."

Dartan glared toward the snake. "I'd bite you if I didn't think the lacuda would attack me the moment my back is turned."

"I'll consider myself grateful we stumbled upon it, then," Aleric shot back. "To think I'm safer with that creature around."

Dartan snorted. "The only way to be safe from a lacuda is if you were still carrying that minky with you."

"I don't get it," Aleric replied. "What does that mean?"

"Surely you've heard the saying; it's a schoolyard chant, for Blays' sake. They swing the ropes and repeat the words to the rhythm...." Dartan waited for Aleric to nod. When the werewolf didn't, he recited, "Frolic in the light of day. Use the sunlight for your play." He paused for a moment, then said, "Something, something...in to stay, or you'll meet the lacuda." He glanced at Aleric. "Ring any bells?"

"I didn't go to school," Aleric said flatly.

"And yet they call you a doctor," Dartan replied. He

shook his head. "What is this world coming to?" He hummed a few bars, then recited, "Frolic in the light of day, use the sunlight for your play, after dark go in to stay, or you'll meet the lacuda."

"Morbid," Aleric said.

Dartan ignored him and continued, "If in the alleys you should go, say bye to the friends you know, prepare you for the ground below, for you'll meet the lacuda."

"That's what school children sing?" Aleric said, appalled. "It makes me grateful I didn't go to school."

"There's more to it," Dartan said. "Stop interrupting. Let me see if I can remember...." He fell silent, hummed a few more bars, then said, "If to the darkness you must go, take a minky for your foe, ensure that the gold eyes glow, and conquer the lacuda."

Aleric waited, but the vampire had stopped speaking. "That's it? Take a minky and you'll be fine?"

"That's how the song goes," Dartan said.

"It sounds like something one person said, he took a minky with him to prove it, and was never heard from again," Aleric pointed out.

Dartan shrugged. "As far as I know, we have a minky and no better idea. It couldn't hurt to try."

Aleric wasn't able to argue the vampire's logic. "Fine. I'll go get the minky," he gave in. "Wait here."

He took several steps toward the mouth of the alley.

"Why do I have to wait here?" Dartan protested with a hint of fear in his voice. He looked between Aleric and the lacuda as if afraid to lose sight of either of them.

"Lilian has to drive given both of our driving history, the minky trusts me, and you're the only one left," Aleric replied. He took several more steps. "I hope you aren't eaten by the time I get back."

"Have I mentioned that I hate you?" Dartan asked.

Aleric grinned and stepped out of the alley with a feeling of relief. He hurried to Lilian's car. Joking aside, he was afraid he would find his friend eaten when he returned. Memories of his childhood haunted his mind. It wouldn't hurt to hurry.

They found Police Commissioner Oaks and several officers waiting at the mouth of the alley when they returned. Officer Ling gave Aleric a friendly nod.

"Is a giant snake really a job for the police?" the Commissioner asked when Aleric climbed out of the car.

"This one is," Aleric told him. "Did you bring the big truck?"

"One of my guys owns a moving company. He's on his way," the Commissioner replied.

Aleric stepped into the alley. His wolven eyesight adjusted quickly to the darkness. Behind him, the click of flashlights sounded and circles of light shone on the walls and alley floor. The high buildings around them cut out the light of the moon overhead.

"This place is creepy," one of the officers said.

"You still here?" Aleric called out as he rounded the corner where he had left Dartan.

Dartan glared back at him. The vampire's eyes shone red in the flashlight beams. Aleric heard the officers' steps slow. Lilian caught up to Aleric and walked beside him.

"I can't believe you left me here with it," Dartan said in an accusing tone when Aleric drew near.

"You have fangs," Aleric pointed out.

"I'm not going to bite a giant snake."

"You would if it attacked you," Aleric said.

Dartan muttered something with the word 'hate' in it and Aleric fought back another grin.

"Officer Ling, if you would be so kind as to shine your

light in that direction," Aleric directed.

The officer did as he was instructed. When the light fell on the gold and black scales visible between the torn bags of garbage, gasps went up through the officers.

"It's huge!" Officer Ling exclaimed as he followed the path of the body through the alley.

Coils rose and fell beneath and above the bags of trash. Aleric had no idea why garbage always seemed to amass in alleys like that one, huge stacks of black, white, and dark green bags whose smell combined to create a bouquet of stench that surpassed even that of the snake. The garbage gave the perfect place for a snake the size of the lacuda to hide.

"Snakes this big don't exist," one of the officers said.

"They do now," Commissioner Oaks replied.

By the tightness of his tone, Aleric knew the Commissioner no long doubted why the werewolf had called him.

Aleric's eyes followed the coils along the path of Officer Ling's flashlight. The body curled around and around, its width in the middle nearly as wide as Lilith was tall.

"Oh no!" she said the moment the officer's flashlight beam reached the head of the snake.

Its green eyes were open and it watched them from a distance of less than ten feet away.

"I've been standing here this close?" Dartan said, his voice tight.

Everyone took several steps back.

At their movement, the snake's head rose. Lilith let out a little squeak of fear when it towered above them. Aleric's heart thundered in his chest. He wondered if he had just brought all of the officers there to become a feast for the huge lacuda. He took a step forward.

"Aleric, what are you doing?" Lilith asked in a loud whisper.

The officers' radios beeped. "The moving truck is here," a female voice said.

Nobody answered.

Aleric swallowed the lump in his throat. "Easy," he said in a low, soothing tone. "Just come with us."

"It's not like it understands what you're saying," Dartan pointed out, his voice tight with fear. "You sound like dinner to that creature."

Aleric kept his gaze on the snake's huge green eyes. The creature's mouth opened and massive fangs longer than Aleric's arm lowered from the roof of its mouth.

"Take it easy," he repeated. "No one's going to hurt you."

"Head back to the car," Dartan said to Lilith. "Slow movements. Get to safety."

When Lilith took a step backwards, the snake moved. The undulating of the coils upset the garbage bags and more of its body was revealed. Aleric could hear the pounding of the officers' hearts behind him. Breaths caught, footsteps shuffled backwards, and prayers and curses were whispered.

"It's worth a try," Aleric said, his voice soft. With shaking fingers, he pulled the minky from his sling.

The little winged cat's purr turned to a hiss of fear when it saw the snake. The lacuda surged forward.

"Uh, Dartan, it's not working!" Aleric called over his shoulder as the creature closed the distance between them. The minky scrambled in an attempt to get free.

Aleric could hear the vampire reciting the chant again. "If to the darkness you must go, take a minky for your foe, ensure that the gold eyes glow, and conquer the lacuda. Shine your lights in the snake's eyes!" the vampire directed.

All beams moved to the creature's face. The snake

continued forward.

"The snake's eyes are green, not gold," Lilith said with fear in her voice.

"Ling, your light!" Aleric shouted.

Officer Ling tossed the flashlight to him. Aleric held the minky in his good hand. He couldn't clear his arm from the sling fast enough. The flashlight would fly past him and strike the snake. The creature would be to him before he could do anything else. They would all become its next meal.

Dartan's hand shot out and caught the flashlight with lightning speed. He set it in Aleric's palm just before the snake reached them. Aleric shone the light on the minky's face. The kitten's golden eyes reflected the beam.

The lacuda stopped short. Its head lifted, then lowered so that it was at eye-level with Aleric and Diablo. Aleric could barely breathe. All it would take is one gulp to finish them and move on to the others. He had heard tales of the crushing power of the snake's insides. They would all be dead within seconds.

The kitten stopped hissing and its puffed out fur and wings settled. To Aleric's surprise, Diablo began to purr again. The snake's mouth closed. It pushed its nose forward until it touched the minky with the gentleness of a summer breeze.

"Back up," Dartan commanded in a whisper. "Move out of his way."

Aleric heard the officers scrambling to get clear. He took a hesitant step back. As soon as he was a foot away from the snake, the creature slithered forward to touch Diablo with its nose again. Its forked tongue grazed the minky's fur. Diablo didn't seem to mind.

Aleric took another step back, then another. He was worried he would trip on the uneven footing the garbage created. With the flashlight in one hand and the kitten in the other, he wouldn't be able to catch himself for fear of breaking contact with the lacuda.

A hand touched his good shoulder, guiding him. "One step at a time," Dartan said quietly.

Confident he wouldn't trip, Aleric continued backwards. The snake's green eyes lost their sharpness as though the animal was hypnotized. Aleric reached the truck. He glanced back to see a huge rectangular storage box. It's only opening was the massive back door that had been pushed up. The officers and Police Commissioner stood clear of the truck, their wide gazes on the lacuda.

"I'm not sure this is a good idea," Dartan said.

"It's our only option," Aleric replied. He took a steeling breath, sat on the edge of the truck's box, then rose to his knees and feet as smoothly as he was able. The snake followed, pushing its nose forward as Aleric made his way backwards.

Aleric circled around when he reached the back so that he was at the door again. Several brave officers lifted the rest of the snake's body inside with careful movements. With its nose on the minky, the creature didn't seem to mind its coils being pressed into the small space until they could shut the door.

"Climb down," Dartan said.

Aleric stepped onto the bumper. The lacuda moved forward as well. He walked back inside the truck and the snake backed up with him.

"If I leave, it's going to throw a fit," Aleric said.

"You can't ride in the back of the truck," Dartan replied.

"I think I have to."

"Not happening," the vampire argued. "That's ridiculous."

Aleric glanced at his friend out of the corner of his eye. "More ridiculous than letting it smash out of this truck and eat everyone in sight? You and I both know it's capable of that."

Silence fell between them.

Aleric raised his voice. "Commissioner Oaks, please shut the door."

"I agree with the vampire," the Commissioner said. "I think this is a horrible idea, Dr. Wolf. There's got to be another way."

"I'll be fine," Aleric replied. "What we don't need is for the lacuda to escape. I've got its attention. Let's keep it that way."

When it was clear Aleric wasn't going to budge, the Commissioner pulled on the strap. The metal door was caught by a pale hand before it closed. Dartan eased it shut so that the bang didn't alarm the lacuda.

"You better be alive when we get there," Dartan called from outside the truck.

"I'll try my best," Aleric whispered.

Chapter Ten

It was a tense, silent drive. By the time they reached the zoo, Aleric's shoulder was so sore from the position that his hand shook and it took all of his concentration to keep the flashlight beam on the minky's eyes. He was relieved when the truck stopped moving.

Dartan immediately called out, "You still in one piece and that piece not in the snake's belly?"

"Hanging in here," Aleric replied.

There was relief in the vampire's voice when he said, "Leave it to the werewolf to survive being trapped in a truck with a two thousand pound snake."

"I can't believe he rode back there," Aleric heard Lilian say. "Why would anyone do that?"

"He's survived his fair share of being stabbed, bitten, and sliced. I suppose a snake isn't too bad compared to that," Dartan answered.

"I suppose," Lilian replied, but there was doubt in her voice.

A deep woman's voice said, "Dr. Wolf, we're going to slide the door up. The truck is backed up to a secure enclosure where the animal will be safe along with everyone else. We just need to get it in there."

"The lacuda will follow him," Dartan said. "Can he get out through that door?"

"Yes," the woman replied. "As soon as it clears the truck, we'll slide the bars shut. If Dr. Wolf can make it to the door, we can let him out and close it again. The snake will be secure."

"Lacuda," Dartan repeated.

"I don't know what that is," the woman said. "Commissioner Oaks said it's a giant snake."

"Bigger than you can imagine," the Commissioner's deep voice replied.

"At least the cage is big enough," Lilian said, her words touched with worry.

"It used to house our tigers before we built their new facility. We had a very escape-prone tiger, hence the bars across the top as well."

Aleric was starting to feel claustrophobic in the box. Given the length and width of the snake, there wasn't much room for anything but standing in the corner. The flashlight he held flickered. The snake blinked, then its eyes locked on the minky once more. Aleric cleared his throat. "Can we postpone the discussion until later? I'd like to get out of here."

"Get him out of there," Dartan repeated.

"Quickly," Lilian urged.

"Dr. Wolf, we'll have you cross the enclosure—"

"I heard," Aleric replied. The scent of the lacuda clogged his nose and filled his lungs with each breath. The inside of the moving truck was stifling. He felt nauseous. "I just need to get out of here."

The sound of the latch sliding open grated loudly inside the box. Someone pushed on the door from the outside.

"It's stuck," a man called out.

"I've got it," Dartan said.

The door slid up. Aleric sucked in a huge gulp of fresh air. A glance to each side showed police officers, zoo workers, Dartan, Lilian, and a thick-set woman with short brown hair. Her shirt said 'Animals aren't the problem' across the front with a picture of a duckling with a soda bottle on its head.

"Hello Dr. Wolf. It's an honor to meet you," the woman said. "I am Regina Dalley, the director of the Edge City Zoo."

"It's an honor to meet you as well," Aleric replied. "I'd shake your hand, but…." He nodded toward Diablo and the flashlight.

"It's an unusual situation to be sure," Regina replied. "I look forward to introducing the first fae creature into our zoo."

"Hopefully you'll still feel that way in a moment," Officer Ling said.

"Step down carefully, Dr. Wolf," Regina instructed, her gaze on the inside of the truck. "I'd like to see what we're dealing with."

"Easy does it," Dartan told him. "Take your time."

Aleric nodded. Careful to keep his focus on Diablo and the flashlight, he stepped backwards onto the bumper, then to the ground. A gasp sounded from the zoo workers when the lacuda's head followed him out.

"It's magnificent," Regina breathed.

"I'll meet you at the door," Dartan said.

Aleric took another step, then realized the snake wasn't watching him. It was looking directly at Regina. A hiss sounded and its eyes narrowed. If it got angry before they could close the gate, there was the possibility the creature could escape beneath the truck if it could fit its body through. Aleric didn't doubt a lacuda that size could also just shove the vehicle out of the way if it wanted.

"It's not watching the cat!" someone said.

"Turn off the lights!" Lilian shouted. "There's no reflection!"

"Do it," Regina ordered.

The lights shut off. Aleric focused the flashlight on the minky's face. With his werewolf eyesight, he saw the lacuda's head turn and its eyes lock onto the winged kitten once more. Aleric could hear the stuttered breathing of the humans behind the bars. All they could see was the golden reflection of the kitten's eyes.

"Is it working?" Commissioner Oaks asked.

"It is," Aleric replied, grateful he could see in the dark.

He took another step backwards and the snake followed. The sound of the gate opening at the other end of the enclosure was a welcome one. He drew steadily closer. As soon as the snake's body cleared the truck, he called out, "Close the bars."

The snake didn't so much as flinch when the bars slammed shut and a lock was placed on the gate with Regina's steady fingers. Aleric had to give her credit for her composure in the darkness given the terror he could hear from the heartbeats and rapid breathing around him.

"About here, Wolfie?" Dartan asked.

"Just about," Aleric replied.

He stepped over the threshold and felt Dartan's hand guide him through the gate. He maneuvered the minky and flashlight carefully to the right and the lacuda followed him from the other side of the bars. Dartan shut the gate far quieter than the other had been.

"Done," the vampire said with a breath of relief.

Aleric kept the flashlight on. "Do you think it'll hold?" he asked, glancing at the bars.

Dartan pulled on one, then another to test their tightness. "They seem secure. There's one way to know for sure." He raised his voice. "Turn on the light."

The lights flipped on, breaking the connection with the minky.

The snake's massive head reared up. It surged around the cage, making a quick circuit of the huge enclosure. The zoo workers and officers stepped back from the bars.

"At least it has more space than in that alley," Officer Ling noted.

Aleric nodded. The lacuda tested the cage in several areas as it made several more circuits. The knowledge that it couldn't escape seemed to calm the creature. Its hectic movements slowed and it began a more thorough exploration of the area, around the massive logs in the middle, through the pond at one end, and ending up coiled near the far bars, its tongue sliding in and out as it tested the scents of the facility.

"It's just beautiful," Regina said from behind Aleric. "Dr. Wolf, how do I thank you for bringing us such a specimen?"

Aleric shook the hand she held out. "Just make sure it doesn't get out. That'll be thanks enough."

"Deal," she said with a wide smile.

Aleric eased his arm back into the sling as they walked to the waiting vehicles. Diablo climbed inside the sling and immediately fell asleep. Aleric wondered if the minky had kept focused on the lacuda to protect him. He felt a surge of gratitude for the small creature.

"Thanks for the flashlight," Aleric said. He tossed it back to Officer Ling.

"I never thought it'd be used for something like that. Good thing the batteries didn't die, right?" the officer replied.

Dartan looked at Aleric with wide eyes as though the vampire hadn't considered the possibility of that happening.

"It flickered once," Aleric said. "That was the longest second of darkness in my life."

Officer Ling chuckled. "You are a braver man than I."

"I doubt that," Aleric replied. He shook the officer's hand. "Catch you some other time. I'm sure the circumstances will be just as crazy."

"I'd be disappointed if they weren't," Officer Ling replied.

"Have you ever seen someone as happy as that director at the sight of the lacuda?" Dartan asked with a tone that said he didn't know how he felt about it.

"You just gave people another reason to visit the zoo," Commissioner Oaks said. "It's a director's dream come true."

"I'm just happy knowing we aren't going to find it in an alley somewhere," Lilian said. She unlocked her car and climbed in.

"Me, too," Aleric agreed. He shook hands with the Commissioner. "Thanks for your help."

"You did the hard work," Commissioner Oaks replied.

"All I know is when you say giant snake next time, I'm sending someone else."

Aleric laughed and slid onto the passenger seat of the car. He was about to pull the door shut when the Commissioner's radio sounded.

"There's word of another break-in at the blood bank, Commissioner."

"Another one?" Aleric asked before the Commissioner could respond.

The huge man glanced at him. "We get hit every couple of months. We don't have any leads. Do you know who might be at fault?"

Aleric looked at Dartan. The vampire's expression was one of trepidation.

"Possibly," Aleric answered. "Mind if we tag along?"

"Go right ahead," the Commissioner answered.

"Now we're investigators. Nice!" Lilian said as she followed the row of police vehicles down the road. "I've always wanted to say I was busy on police business."

Dartan chuckled. "That does sound official."

They pulled up to the donation center to find reporters and television vans already out front.

Aleric was worried the commotion would scare Diablo, so he slipped off his sling and set the sleeping kitten on the passenger seat.

"We'll be back soon," Aleric said.

Diablo raised her head for a moment, then lowered it again and closed her eyes, comfortably nestled in the folds of the sling.

"Great," Commissioner Oaks muttered as he led the way to the doors. "How do they always know? I swear they're notified before I am."

A man with short gray hair hurried over to meet them.

"How many bags of blood were taken this time, Commissioner?"

"How many bags?" Dartan asked quietly.

"That's the problem," the Commissioner said over his shoulder to them. "We're losing hundreds of bags with each break-in. If it was a dozen or so, the media wouldn't care, but with the amount stolen, we're hard-pressed to keep up with the demand."

He turned back to the reporter. "I don't have specifics at this time."

"Commissioner, do you feel that the break-ins are linked?" a woman Aleric recognized from the Capitol Building gargoyle incident asked.

"We don't know for sure, Gayle. If we find a link, we'll let you know."

Gayle's gaze locked on Aleric and her eyes widened. "Dr. Wolf! What brings you to this investigation? Do they feel there may be a fae element involved with the break-ins?"

Caught off-guard, Aleric looked at the Commissioner. The huge man lifted his shoulders in a barely perceptible shrug. Aleric turned back to the reporter. "Well, Gayle, as Commissioner Oaks said, we don't have a lead yet, but if there is a fae involved, we're prepared to offer one hundred percent support into reaching the bottom of this investigation."

"Thank you, Dr. Wolf," she said.

Other reporters had rushed over during the brief interview. Cell phones and hand-held recorders were shoved toward Aleric.

"Dr. Wolf, do you feel this may be the act of more demons in Edge City?"

"Dr. Wolf, what kind of fae requires so much blood?"

"Dr. Wolf, does Edge City have reason to fear another

fae entity?"

Aleric could tell the Commissioner was about to call off the questioning, but the werewolf saw an opportunity to attempt to make a difference for Perry and the other fae caught on the other side of the Rift. He held up a hand and everyone quieted.

"I don't know who or what is behind the break-ins at the Edge City blood banks, but what I do know is that if it is fae related, there is a reason behind it. The fae who find themselves on the other side of the Rift between our worlds are often scared, sometimes injured, and the majority of them are just looking for a way back home." He felt every camera fix on him. He hoped he looked far more composed then he felt at addressing a television audience. "Edge City is a huge, amazing place, but it can be scary at times."

Aleric saw several people nod out of the corner of his eye. He continued, "I've done and continue to do what I can to keep this city as safe as if it was my own home." Smiles spread across the faces of a few reporters. "I love Edge City and the people here. I find myself growing fonder of your beautiful city with every new day, and I know there are fae who feel the same way. We don't mean any harm to you and your loved ones, and if we can all find a way to live in peace, we can make this city even greater." He smiled. "You've seen my willingness to sacrifice to protect you. Trust me when I say that this vigilance will continue. No matter what the source of fear in this city, I pledge to get to the bottom of it and ensure that Edge City is a safe place for your children to play and grow. Together, we can help Edge City rise to a new level of freedom and security."

Nods and pleased expressions came from the reporters who watched him.

"That was Dr. Wolf from Edge City Hospital addressing

us from the scene of the blood bank robbery," Gayle said to her camera. "We will notify you of further details on the robbery as they arise. Thank you for watching, and goodnight."

Other reporters signed off to their stations. Aleric turned away with the hope that his words would at least ease some of the tension between the citizens and the fae. If they could learn to trust each other, it would go far toward helping the plights of Perry and others who had found happiness after traversing the Rift.

"That was quite the speech," the Commissioner said.

Aleric couldn't tell by his expression how the man felt about his words.

"I didn't mean to make it so dramatic," Aleric replied.

"You have a flare for it," Dartan noted from the Commissioner's other side.

"This coming from a vampire," Aleric said dryly.

Lilian touched Aleric's arm. "It was great."

Commissioner Oaks nodded. "Don't apologize. I feel your words were necessary. Anything that can help ease the fear of fae in this city is a good thing. They see something like this and the media has a field day speculating about the type of creature involved." He took a steeling breath and pushed open the door. "The problem is that I can't figure out who it would be otherwise. What kind of fae needs so much blood?"

Aleric saw Dartan's shoulders tense at the scent of blood that rushed out from the open door. He glanced at his friend, wondering when the vampire had last eaten.

Dartan's jaw was locked and his red gaze stayed carefully impassive. Aleric was reminded of the time Dartan had laid on his back in the demon's lair watching the sunrise. He had chosen to slowly, painfully starve to death instead of taking the blood Aleric had offered. Aleric didn't doubt his friend's control, but the scent of blood was even overwhelming to his werewolf senses; he couldn't imagine how the vampire felt.

"Do you want to wait in the car?" Aleric asked quietly.

Dartan shook his head. "I'm fine."

Lilian glanced back at them and gave them a reassuring smile. If she felt the same worry, she didn't show it.

"As you can see, we're missing even more than before," a man in a white lab coat said.

Aleric turned his attention to the refrigeration room they had entered.

"They took the red cell bags of every blood type," the man continued, showing the big gap along the shelves where the blood bags used to be. "By our count, one hundred and fifteen bags were taken."

"What about the cameras?" the Commissioner asked.

"Knocked out, same as at the North Bank," the man replied.

An officer approached them. "We've checked for prints, Commissioner. Not a trace; just like last time."

Commissioner Oaks looked at Aleric. "Care to sweep the area?"

"Could I have the room for a minute?" he asked. "It's cold enough that the scent might be hard to find. The fewer people in the same area, the better."

"Of course," the Commissioner replied. At his motion, everyone filed out of the huge room. The Commissioner pulled the door shut. "Take your time," he called through it.

Lilian rubbed her arms. "It's a bit chilly."

Aleric crossed to her. "Would you be more comfortable outside?"

She shook her head. "We're investigators, remember?" she asked with a teasing smile. "Let's get investigating."

"Go to it, Wolfie," Dartan said. "Good luck smelling

anything in here."

Aleric took off his shirt. A shiver ran across his bare skin. He phased into wolf form, grateful to have the thick, warm coat to protect him. He padded to the shelves, sniffing the floor as he went.

"The great fae bloodhound," Dartan said to Lilian. "If the Commissioner knew he had a doctor *and* a hound in this one, he might not let the hospital have him back."

Lilian laughed. "They could change his name to Sherlock Bones."

"I like that," Dartan replied. "What do you think, Wolfie?"

Aleric snorted.

Dartan laughed in response. "He's a hound of few words."

Aleric pushed their banter to the background and concentrated on the matter at hand. Dartan was right; finding a fae scent in the cold room would be a difficult task. If they hadn't located any fingerprints, there was the chance whoever it was had been careful enough not to touch anything that might also leave a smell on the—

Aleric paused. He checked the shelf again. There it was, faint, nearly a day old, but the scent he had been both hoping and fearing to find. The vampiress.

Aleric followed the scent to the door. Now that he knew what he was looking for, it was easier to locate.

"You found it?" Dartan said in surprise. "Now what?"

At Aleric's expectant look, the vampire put a hand on the door. "Fine, but you're going to rush through a mess of officers and reporters. You'll have to get out of here quickly. Figure out where she took the blood, but don't be a hero. Come get us before you confront her. We need somewhere to meet up."

"Meet at my place," Lilian said.

"Wolfie's been to your place?" Dartan replied.

Red colored Lilian's cheeks. "We were getting a tent for the grims."

"Oh. Right. That's what they all say," the vampire replied. He touched her cheek with a finger. "You're quite attractive when you blush, you know." He winked at her. "Especially to a vampire. Did you know blushing is caused by a widening of the blood vessels of your face which increases blood flow to your skin? It's quite striking."

Aleric gave a short growl.

Dartan lifted his hands. "Alright, alright! I wasn't going to do anything, I swear."

Lilian giggled.

Dartan grinned at Aleric. "I can't help it if the woman you're sweet on knows how to push a vampire's buttons. I don't know what she sees in you, Fuzzy."

Aleric growled again.

"Go," Dartan said with a hand on the door. "Run. I promise we'll meet you at Lilian's with her in as gorgeous of a shape as she is right now."

As anxious as he was to get on with the hunt for the vampiress, he wasn't thrilled about leaving Lilian with Dartan. But the moment the vampire opened the door, the officers were there.

"Did you find anything?" Commissioner Oaks asked.

Aleric couldn't chance them trailing him to the vampiress before he could ascertain her intentions in Edge City. If Dartan was right about the power and greed of a vampiress, others could be in danger.

Aleric burst past the officers and took off running for the outer door. An officer stood there talking to one of the donation center workers. When he saw Aleric loping up the hallway, he pushed the door open. Aleric flew threw.

"Follow him!" Commissioner Oaks commanded.

Aleric was around the side of the building and following the vampiress' trail through the darkness before either the reporters or officers could react.

"Any idea where he's going?" he heard the Commissioner ask.

"I think he saw a cat," Dartan replied.

Aleric rolled his eyes and continued his run through the dark alleys of Edge City.

Chapter Eleven

"You tracked the vampiress to a scary underground lair, and now you expect us to follow?" Dartan asked in an incredulous tone.

"You told me not to be a hero and to come get you," Aleric reminded him.

"I think I prefer to stay here. Go ahead and be a hero. You seem to be good at it," Dartan replied. He looked comfortable sprawled on Dr. Worthen's couch. "Think we can get them to move this to the Dark fae wing of the hospital? I doubt Dr. Worthen would notice it's gone. He's hardly here."

Lilian chuckled. "That's Dad's favorite couch. I find him here sleeping more often than his bed. He'd definitely notice. Now let's go."

"You seriously want to follow this werewolf to a vampiress' lair? You really don't know what you're getting into."

"It sounds like you don't, either," Aleric said. He straightened his shirt and stepped into his shoes. His shoulder gave a twinge and he rubbed it, willing the ache to stop. The run had definitely been hard on the wound that refused to heal completely despite so much time beneath the full moon. "You said vampiresses were rare in Blays because they killed each other off. Have you ever actually met one?"

Dartan gave Aleric a wide-eyed look. "Are you saying I haven't met a vampiress?"

"That's exactly what I'm saying," Aleric replied, his tone flat. "Don't be dramatic and admit it."

Dartan glared at the ceiling from his spot on the couch.

"Have you met one?" Lilian prompted.

Dartan glanced at her out of the corner of his eye. "Not in the shaking her hand and signing off my soul to the devil form of meet," he admitted.

"What other kind of meet is there?" Aleric asked.

"Elk, buffalo. I hear faun is a bit gamey."

Aleric opened the front door. "If you're going to sit here stalling until the sun rises and you can't go out, fine. I've got an elf's life to save."

Diablo ran up to the door and pawed at Aleric's pant leg. He picked up the meowing minky.

"Stay here. You'll be safe. Lilian and I will pick you up as soon as we're done, I promise," he said, petting the kitten's head. He set her on the arm of the couch.

"This is ridiculous," Dartan said, rising to his feet. "Who ever heard of a werewolf with a pet minky?" He looked at Lilian. "I don't think we have a real werewolf. We've been swindled."

"By whom?" she asked with a smile.

"Don't encourage him," Aleric told her. "He's just trying to find a way out of this."

"You'll thank me if you don't go, trust me," Dartan replied.

He was still repeating the words as he followed Aleric and Lilian down the subway tunnel beneath the city.

"Now look, it's dark and scary. She really knows how to set her ambiance," Dartan muttered.

"What do you expect?" Aleric asked. "And you're the scariest thing down here."

"Don't be so sure about that," Dartan replied.

Lilian's hand slipped into Aleric's. He smiled at her and heard her breath catch.

"What is it?" he asked with concern.

"Oh, sure. Worry about her," Dartan said.

They both ignored him.

"Your eyes reflected my flashlight beam," she told him. "I didn't expect that."

Aleric nodded. "That's part of the wolf trait. I can see better in the dark even in this form. It sticks around from my wolf side."

"He smells in the dark, too," Dartan said. "That's another wolf trait." The tightness of his voice told of how nervous he was despite his joking. "Don't let him out in the rain. The wet dog smell is hard to get off the furniture."

"What about you?" Lilian asked Dartan. "Do vampires have attributes other than the need to drink blood that set them apart from humans?"

"Speed," Aleric and Dartan said at the same time.

At Lilian's questioning expression, Dartan explained, "My reflexes are faster. It's a survival trait of ours. I'm also stronger, but using speed or strength takes up extra blood, so I reserve it until I need it." He winked at her. "We're also a handsomer race as a whole. I don't know if you've noticed; the difference is subtle."

"Oh, is it?" Lilian said with her teasing smile. "I hadn't noticed."

Dartan put a hand to his heart. "You scald me with your cruel words," he said dramatically.

The trail led Aleric to a panel in the wall. He pushed against it, but the stone panel didn't budge.

"How about using some of that strength now?" he suggested, stepping aside.

Dartan gave the brick subway wall a skeptical look. "You really think there's someone hiding behind here?"

"If there is, they chose a place not many could follow," Aleric replied.

Dartan's face was somber as he pushed against the stone. The muscles in his neck and arms strained, but the panel didn't move. He finally gave up. "There must be a catch somewhere. It's too heavy, even for me."

"What about that?"

Aleric and Dartan followed Lilian's gaze to a small piece of blue ribbon just visible from a hole in the mortar. Lilian pulled on it. A barely audible click sounded. Aleric put a hand to the panel and the door swung inward with the lightest touch.

"Clever," he said.

"Leave it to a female to use lace as a key," Dartan said.

"Ribbon," Lilian corrected. "The difference is subtle."

Dartan's mouth fell open.

Aleric snorted. "Get it right, Toothy."

"I'm feeling ganged up on," the vampire replied.

He led the way down a set of narrow stairs.

"Is this feeling a bit creepy cliché to anyone else?" Dartan asked.

"Me," Lilian said.

"Me, too," Aleric echoed.

He had to admit that the chill in the air, the scent of the vampiress and the blood bags, and the way the door closed behind him set the ambiance a bit too murderous for his liking. He hoped he was correct about the vampiress' good intentions. Their brief introduction in the forest near Fabien's shack hadn't left time to truly understand anything about her. For all he knew, he was leading his friends into a trap. He paused in front of the door at the bottom of the stairs.

"Maybe you guys should wait a bit further up," he suggested. "I could be wrong."

"Now you admit it," Dartan said. He shook his head. "There's no way we're letting you go in alone. Besides, she could just as easily come down these stairs behind us and we'd be trapped."

"Good point," Aleric conceded.

"Together, then?" Lilian said. Her voice shook slightly. "Let's meet this wench."

Dartan lifted his hand to the door with a chuckle. "She said wench," he told Aleric. "I'm liking her more and more."

The vampire touched the wood frame and the door swung inward. Everyone stared.

Aleric wasn't sure what he had expected. Something in the form of a torch-lit torture chamber perhaps, with stone beds, plenty of spikes, a few humans chained to walls for the vampiress to drink from, and maybe an actual pit of despair— he had always wanted to see one of those.

Instead, tasteful beige couches sat on thick white carpets, black curtains hung to the sides of long, elegant mirrors, and a dining room table held one place setting near the far end of the room. Across from it, a four-poster bed was hung with red and black curtains, a nightstand held a beautiful silver candelabra, and everything glowed with soft, recessed lighting from the ceiling above.

"Did we go through the right door?" Dartan asked. He stepped back out to the stairs, looked around, and came back in. "It's the only one. I thought it couldn't hurt to check."

Aleric crossed into the room. He pushed down the urge to take off his shoes to avoid getting the white carpets dirty.

"This is where the trail leads," he told them. "The blood must be here."

"Of course it's here."

Everyone started at the vampiress' voice even though it was spoken barley above a whisper.

She stepped into view from a room that branched off of the main one. Her purple gaze swept over them. "What do you think I subside on? Sewer rats?"

"I wouldn't put it past you, Vampiress," Dartan said, his tone reproving.

"I'll admit, I've consisted on my fair share of them," she said, walking toward the trio. "For survival only, until I found a better source."

"You've been raiding the blood banks," Dartan accused.

"Do you suggest I go with far more deadly tactics to get what I need?" the vampiress asked, her tone light but with a hint of steel. "At least this blood is donated, not taken by force." She was nearly to them, her fierce gaze locked on the vampire's.

"You're younger than I expected," Dartan said, his voice filled with accusation as he crossed to meet her. "You don't appear much older than me."

Fearing a fight that would destroy what they had come to do, Aleric stepped between them.

"Is that a problem?" the vampiress asked, stopped inches from the werewolf.

"There are no young vampiresses in Blays," Dartan pointed out.

"Of course not," the vampiress replied. "They kill each other off. Why do you think I'm here?"

"You're hiding out?" Dartan asked. "Cowering?"

"Call it what you will," the vampiress said. "I haven't had a fresh meal in decades." She leaned toward Aleric, her fangs bared. "What's to keep me from partaking of the werewolf here?"

Aleric's muscles tensed, but he didn't move. Instincts told him that to run meant to die. Dartan said vampiresses were far stronger. Any wrong move could bring death to them all. He was getting a little tired of that scenario.

"If you wanted a live meal, you wouldn't be stealing blood bags," Dartan said.

The vampiress paused. Aleric could feel the warmth of her breath against the skin of his neck.

"My blood tastes like wet dog."

Silence filled the room. It was broken by the vampiress' laughter. She put a delicate hand on Aleric's shoulder.

"Who told you that?" she asked, her voice musical with mirth.

"Dartan. I was dying on an operating table. He muttered it after telling the nurses what blood type I needed in order to save my life."

Dartan looked truly appalled. "I didn't know you heard that." He held up a hand. "To be fair, I was about to lose my best friend. I can't be held responsible for anything I said."

The vampiress stared at them both. "You're best friends?"

"Hard to believe, right?" Lilian asked.

The vampiress looked at the human and her gaze softened. "I heard them fighting on their way down the stairs. No wonder. You're gorgeous! They should be fighting over you."

"They weren't fighting over—"

"Come get warm," the vampiress said, cutting off her reply. "It's freezing out there." Lilian gave Aleric and Dartan a little helpless shrug as she was led past them by the vampiress. "I apologize for my inhospitable entrance. It's hard to find privacy in a city like this. I've had to make due."

"You make due very well," Lilian replied. "This place is beautiful."

The vampiress smiled as she sat beside Lilian near the happily dancing fire in a brickwork fireplace. A closer look revealed that it was powered by a propane tank hidden artfully behind a decorative end table.

"I don't have many visitors," the vampiress said. "Actually none since I've been here."

"How long have you lived here?" Lilian asked.

"Decades. I've lost count."

Dartan cleared his throat at the vampiress' answer. "The Rift has only been here a few weeks." He paused at the vampiress' glance and ended with, "Uh, Miss."

"Call me Vallia," the vampiress said. She extended a hand. Dartan hurried over to it, bowed, and kissed the back of it as though he was a suitor at a ball from a time long past.

"Dartan Targeshson. It's a pleasure to meet you."

"The pleasure is mine," the vampiress replied.

Aleric and Lilian exchanged surprised looks.

"I didn't come through the Rift," the vampiress

continued. "Though I've seen signs of your entrance to this city." She met Aleric's gaze. "I've hidden here alone for such a great amount of time that I became curious about a fae so actively involved in helping the humans. I followed you."

"And saved me when the gorgons attacked," Aleric said. "That's actually why we're here. I need another antidote like the one you gave me."

"The gorgons have bitten someone else?" Vallia replied in surprise.

"An elf," Aleric told her. "A woodland elf, to be exact. I'm afraid she's weakening at the hospital from the effects of the bite as we speak. She doesn't have much time left. Can you help?"

The vampiress had risen at Aleric's words and was already pulling vials from a bookshelf near her dining table. The speed with which she worked made it hard to follow her actions.

"You said you've been here decades," Dartan said. "How is that possible?"

"My mother left me at Edge City when I was nine with nothing but a book on potions and this place in which to hide," Vallia replied without looking at him. "She feared for my safety and felt it was the only way I would survive."

"There's another Rift?" Dartan said in shock. "Do you know where it is?"

Vallia paused and looked at him; the dancing light of the fire reflected in her sad, purple gaze. "I've searched for it my entire life."

Dartan's tone was unreadable when he said, "Why look for it when going home would mean your death?"

Vallia turned back to her work. "Sometimes facing down death is a better option than living a life that impacts no other. Loneliness can be far more painful than not existing at all. I had to try."

"We could help you get back," Aleric offered. "It might be safer now."

Vallia shook her head. "There's danger coming. I don't know how, but it's drawing near. I can feel it. I need to stay."

Aleric opened his mouth to argue, but Dartan shook his head.

"A vampire's instincts are something never to argue against," the vampire said. "We'll respect your wish."

"Thank you," Vallia replied. She handed Aleric the vial she had mixed. "This should help the elf if it was indeed a gorgon that bit her."

The thought seemed to bother the vampiress a great deal. When she walked them back to the door through which they had come, she had a pensive look on her face. "I wish you all the best of luck."

"The same to you," Aleric told her. "Thank you for your hospitality."

"Thank you for making me laugh," she replied with a kind smile. "It's been a long time."

The werewolf and vampire reached the stairs.

"Please come by to visit any time," Vallia told Lilian. "I would love to have a friend here, especially a female. Sometimes it would be nice to have some girl talk."

"I would like that," Lilian replied. "Thank you for your kindness."

Dartan chuckled as they walked through the subway passage. "That was not what I expected at all," he said.

"She was very sweet. I'll definitely take her up on her offer. I could use a friend to talk to myself," Lilian mused.

"I'm a friend," Dartan pointed out.

Lilian smiled at him. "I mean a girl. It's different."

"I could pretend to like shiny things, pictures of cats, and chocolate," Dartan replied.

"Chocolate?" Aleric repeated.

"Dreadful stuff. Sticks to my teeth, and you know how I feel about my teeth," Dartan said. "On second thought, hang out with Vallia."

Lilian laughed. Aleric was about to join in when a sound caught his ear. He held up a hand.

"What's that?" Dartan asked. "You have a question? I thought our friendship was a bit less formal than that, although your politeness is to be commended—"

"I heard something," Aleric replied, cutting him off.

"We'd better listen," Dartan said in a mockingly loud undertone to Lilian. "This one has sonar hearing."

"Seriously?" Aleric said.

Dartan held up his hands. "Fine. Listen away. If your hearing's so good, why can't you hear over us, huh?" At Aleric's look, the vampire quieted.

In the silence, the sound Aleric had heard intensified.

"There's fighting ahead." He took off running.

"Why are we running toward the fighting?" Dartan asked, chasing after him.

"Have you ever heard of people fighting this early in the morning?" Aleric called over his shoulder.

"It's just before five o'clock," Lilian said, catching up to them both. "What would they have to fight about?"

"I think I might know." Aleric led the way up the stairs from the subway tunnel and paused on the steps above the road.

A brawl took up most of the street. Nearly a hundred people threw punches, kicked, bit, slapped, screamed, yelled, cried, and argued. The sun was just showing as a gray wisp of dawn caught in the high windows of the buildings around them. The people looked poorly suited to be fighting in the streets. Most of them were in their underwear, nightgowns, sweats, and a few were completely naked.

"It looks like they woke up and came to brawl," Lilian said, her eyes wide. "I've never seen anything like it."

"That's ridiculous," Dartan said from Aleric's other side. "What could cause this much chaos?" The vampire lifted his voice and shouted, "Hey! Knock it off!"

The fighting continued as if his words didn't matter.

"I know of only one person who could infuse so many people with the will to battle." Aleric cupped his hands around his mouth. The howl he let out was long and angry. It tore from his chest and echoed along the brick buildings.

The sound was so unexpected amid the brawl that the humans below slowed, then stopped entirely. The crowd looked at each other with baffled expressions. Eyes were blackening and noses streamed blood from faces that took on apologetic expressions. Startled exclamations and apologies sounded.

"Wallace!" Aleric shouted. "Show yourself!"

A moment later, the clop of hooves was heard. A man appeared at the corner on a blood-red horse. He held a sword of fire in his hand. Gasps sounded from the crowd; the humans pushed against the buildings on either side to make room for him.

"Why does Aleric know the Horseman of War by his first name?" the werewolf heard Dartan whisper to Lilian.

"I have no idea," she whispered back with shock in her voice.

Aleric walked down two steps and paused so that he was eye-level with the horseman. He had to admit that Wallace made an impressive sight, his red mount pawing at the pavement while the sword of flames crackled and glowed in the early daylight.

"I saw that you were in town, Aleric," the horseman said in a tone of camaraderie that chased away the intimidation of his appearance.

"What are you doing?" Aleric demanded.

Wallace looked around at the people. The sight of the bloody faces and bruised knuckles made his mouth turn up at one corner. "I don't see a problem."

Aleric glared at him. "You invoked a riot in people who were asleep, not to mention you stole Fluffy. Why put your brother through that?"

"Who's Fluffy?" Dartan whispered.

"Fabien's horse," Lilian replied from behind Aleric.

Wallace looked surprised. "I didn't steal Fluffy. Why would I do that?"

His reply caught Aleric off-guard. "To cause chaos, like you do." He waved at the crowd to confirm his point.

Wallace glanced behind him. "I might enjoy a little ruckus, but I know better than to torment Fabien. He loves that horse more than he does any of us." He patted his great red steed's neck. "Who could blame him, right Bob?"

Aleric shook his head, confused. "If you weren't the one who forced Fabien to poison the tomatoes so Perry's business got shut down, who would do it? Who here even knows the Horsemen exist?"

"Hey!" Wallace protested.

"It's true," Aleric replied. "The Horsemen might be legend here, but you really belong to Blays." He indicated the dispersing crowd of humans. Confusion showed clearly on their faces as to why they had been brawling in the street. "Look at them. They aren't warriors. They aren't born with fighting blood for you to boil and fill with rage. They're businessmen and women, homemakers, doctors, lawyers, peaceful citizens for the most part. This isn't fair to them."

The Third Horseman studied the faces of the people who kept as far from him and his horse as possible as they returned to their apartments. Lines of apology traced his face.

"I believe you're right." He watched them a moment longer before he turned back to Aleric. "That settles it. I intend to return home to Blays, and I hear you've a way to do just that."

Aleric nodded. "I do."

Wallace patted his horse's shoulder with a flourish. "It's done. I'll round up my brothers and we'll head back to where we belong."

A thought occurred to Aleric. "You might want to leave Perry here. He seems happy with his restaurant."

A smile spread across Wallace's face as though Aleric's words gave him great joy. "I'll do that. It's about time that boy got to live out his dreams. I'm sure Fabien will be eager to go back, but I don't know about Doyle. He disappeared the moment we got here. He can't leave without her, you know."

Aleric had no idea what the Horseman was talking about. "Who do you mean?"

"Haga," Wallace said. "She's Doyle's girlfriend. She's the reason we're all here. She disappeared, so Doyle insisted we all come to find her, but this place is like looking for a sand wisp in a flock of pixies. I figured if I could create a little trouble, it might stir her up. But as you can see, no Haga."

"Would Doyle take Fluffy?" Aleric thought it was perhaps the craziest question he had ever asked. Had the Horseman of Death taken his kid brother's beloved pet? It sounded petty to be sure, but Aleric was running out of conclusions.

"Possibly, I suppose," Wallace replied in a doubtful tone. "He wouldn't do it out of spite, to be sure." The Third

Horseman looked at Lilian. "Considering the fact that he's Death, he's not very spiteful. I always tell him to mix it up a bit, but Doyle's pretty level-headed in view of his occupation."

"I'm glad to hear that," Lilian replied in a hesitant tone as if she wasn't exactly sure what to say in that particular situation.

Wallace watched the last of the humans disappear inside the nearby apartment complexes. He let out a sigh. "Well, I'm done here. I'll go round up Fabian and say goodbye to Perry. If we can find Fluffy, we'll meet you at the back of the hospital you seem to call home, Aleric. I'm guessing you see the irony in that. I love irony." He grinned and clicked his tongue. His horse trotted up the road. "I miss good battles with steel and sweat, blood and brawn," he called over his shoulder. "It'll be good to return to Blays. I'm quite fond of the place."

He spurred Bob into a gallop and vanished around the corner.

Chapter Twelve

Dr. Worthen hurried out to meet them as soon as Lilian pulled up to the hospital.

"You brought it!" he exclaimed. "Thank goodness." He gave his daughter a hug. "I was beginning to worry that they had run off with you for good." He eyed the vampire and werewolf with only a half-smile to alleviate his stern glare.

"They're not so bad," Lilian replied.

Dartan excused himself as they made their way to the elf's room. "Needless to say, the night's activities have spiked my hunger. There's nothing like a donation center to provoke the appetite. I'll excuse myself." He nudged Aleric in the ribs. "I also have a very early morning date with Dr. Indley."

"I'm happy for you," Aleric told the vampire.

The elf looked far worse than she had when Aleric left. The silver leaf markings across her skin were almost lost in her gray pallor. Her breaths came in short gasps and her pulse was slower than before.

Dr. Worthen gave his head a small shake. "I've never seen a stomach wound heal with such speed while the rest of her deteriorates so fast I feared she wouldn't be alive when you returned. Here's to hoping we aren't too late."

Dr. Worthen injected the antidote. Lilian and Aleric watched the elf with bated breaths. Aleric wondered when Lilian's fingers had slipped into his. He was worried Dr. Worthen would notice, but didn't want to let go.

When the elf's condition didn't change, Dr. Worthen let out a sigh. "I suppose we'll have to be patient. I'll have Nurse Tarli notify us if there's any improvement." He glanced at Aleric as they followed him out of the room. "She's threatening to call animal control on your cat. She says even though he's a patient, he should have been sent to Dr. Indley's veterinary clinic instead of here."

"The sphinx is safer here than out there. We'll get him through the Rift as soon as we can," Aleric promised. "She can't expect us to throw him out on the streets."

"You know she expects exactly that," Dr. Worthen replied in a droll tone. "Speaking of cats, I've heard a lot about the, uh, minky, is it?"

"Diablo!" Aleric and Lilian said at the same time. They shared matching expressions of guilt.

"I thought she was sweeter than that," Dr. Worthen replied in surprise.

"That's her name," Lilian replied. "And we accidentally

left her at the house. We need to go get her."

"At our house?" Dr. Worthen repeated in an uncertain tone. "Why were you at our house?"

Lilian looked at Aleric. "It's a long story," she said.

Dr. Worthen glanced at their hands. Lilian let go quickly. Her father's expression became unreadable.

"We'll be back soon, Dad. I promise."

"I'm not sure about this," Dr. Worthen began.

Lilian kissed him on the cheek. "Don't worry, Dad. It's okay. We'll be back, alright?"

They crossed through the hospital toward the back parking lot where Lilian had parked her car. Dartan stepped out of the D Wing with a bag of blood.

"We need to talk, Wolfie," he said.

Aleric had a feeling he knew exactly what the vampire wanted to discuss.

"Don't you have a date with Dr. Indley?" he asked, hoping for a way out. "I bet there'll be a better time to talk later when we aren't interrupting your wooing." He almost succeeding in saying the last work without chuckling. Lilian laughed at his side.

Dartan crossed his arms in front of his chest. "She had an emergency surgery show up. Now is the perfect time."

"I'm exhausted," Aleric told his friend. "We need to go get Diablo, then I've got to get some sleep before I crash. It's been a long night. Also, the day before that was long, and the night before that. It's been long since I reached this place."

"This is important," the vampire replied.

Dartan put a hand on both Aleric and Lilian's shoulders and steered them into the Dark fae side of the D Wing.

The absence of the plague victims was a relief. I.V. poles stood in a straight row against the far wall. Dartan's tables where he had extracted the goblin bite antidotes were clean and empty. Only the faint scent of mud and lemon along with the stronger odor of sulfur remained to remind Aleric of what had gone on in that room.

"It's quiet in here," he noted.

"I like it that way," Dartan replied. "Will you stop filling this place with things that try to kill me?"

"You're already dead," Aleric said.

Dartan sighed and slid to his usual place on the floor beneath one of the boarded up windows.

"Come. Sit. Enjoy my happy place," he told them.

Lilian gave the dark, partially-finished room a skeptical look as she crossed it. "This is your happy place?"

Dartan nodded. "That's why I'm so cheerful."

She smiled and took a seat on the floor near him. At the vampire's look, Aleric sat down as well.

"You could use a couch in here," Lilian said.

"I tried to borrow your father's, remember? Tell him it's a worthy cause," Dartan replied.

Aleric leaned back against the wall. He closed his eyes. It felt nice to relax after everything that had happened. If the others were to stop talking, he was sure he would fall asleep in an instant.

"How do you know the Four Horsemen on a first name basis?"

Dartan's question made his eyes open again. Aleric looked at the vampire. It was clear by his friend's expression that Dartan knew exactly what a first name basis with those type of fae meant. He wasn't going to get out of the discussion easily.

A pit tightened in Aleric's stomach. He looked at Lilian. "I'm not sure you want to hear this."

"You're not sure I want to hear this or not sure you want me to hear this?" Lilian asked. When he didn't reply, she set a hand on his arm. "Aleric, I feel like I need to know. You've been through things I can't begin to understand. Let me in. Let me know."

Aleric shook his head and turned his gaze to the floor. "It won't be easy to hear."

"I think it'll be worth it," she replied, her voice gentle and hand warm on his skin.

Aleric closed his eyes again, but it wasn't to escape the world in which he sat. It was to remember, and the memories that flooded behind his eyelids were things he had pushed down so hard seeing them again nearly broke him. He squeezed his eyes with his hand, willing the tears to stay at bay. He had forbidden them back then. He would do so again.

"Tell us." Dartan's words were soft, imploring.

Aleric knew he owed his friend the truth.

He pulled his knees up under his chin, unseating Lilian's hand on purpose. He didn't want to be touched, not by her, not by anyone. He didn't deserve it, and she would soon know why.

He met her gaze. Her blue eyes were searching and depthless, her brow furrowed in her want to understand. There was love in that gaze. The realization caught Aleric by surprise. She cared about him. It might not be the same way he felt for her, but it was there, emotion, understanding, compassion, and respect.

Aleric swallowed. He would never see that look on her face again.

He cleared his throat. "After the Fallow Conflict, when all of the werewolves in Blays were killed including my dear friend Sherian, I didn't have much of a choice left." He glanced at Dartan. "Vampires and demons scoured the streets at night hunting for any of us who remained. The fae I had called friends betrayed me for money and the safety of their families. I had nowhere to go. Everyone I knew was dead. I wanted to die."

His breath caught at that admission. Dartan and Lilian waited without speaking for him to collect his thoughts. Aleric shook his head. "But I couldn't." He spoke to the floor, his gaze on a crack in the tile near his shoe. "A werewolf's instincts refuse to let him or her give up. We can't take our own life. I couldn't sit and wait for them to find me." He looked at them both, willing them to understand. "We have to fight, to survive, to uphold our race even if it's against our own demand." His voice dropped to a whisper. "Our race must go on."

The silence that pressed against Aleric came from every side. It felt heavy, depressing, holding him down, daring him to break it. It was a few moments before he could bring himself to do so.

"I went back to my animal nature, as others of my kind have done in desperate times. I became a wolf and only a wolf. I ran through the forests of Blays as an animal, eating, hunting, sleeping as a wolf until I no longer thought as a human, until the memories were distant and I could sleep without awakening with the nightmare of finding my friends and pack mates slain in their beds, holding my loved ones' bodies while their lifeblood colored the floor at my feet."

He remembered the green light. "I don't know how they found me. I remember awakening in a cage surrounded by creatures in black cloaks." He looked at Lilian, his gaze haunted. "I call them creatures because they weren't human and they weren't animal. They had abnormally long arms and legs, their noses stretched into beaks and cowls over their heads to hide the hideousness of their faces."

"The Drakathan." Dartan said the word with barely a

breath as though fearing that to say it would bring them there. Aleric knew his fears were justified.

The werewolf nodded. "The Drakathan. The darkest of the Dark fae. The devourers of souls, the anti-destiny, the enders of the path."

Into the silence that followed, Lilian repeated, "The anti-destiny?"

Aleric met her gaze. "They don't care if someone is good or bad, how their path is affecting people, if they have a family to feed, others who depend on them for sustenance or care. All they care about is themselves."

"The Drakathan," Dartan said again. There was a note to his words and an incomprehension to the way he repeated them. "You were found by the Drakathan."

Aleric looked at his friend. "My soul must be pretty dark to have attracted them to me."

Dartan shook his head. He rose to his feet. "I know that's not true. Just promise me you aren't pledged to them."

The werewolf looked away.

"Aleric!" Dartan said, his voice sharp. When the werewolf didn't answer, Dartan repeated, "Aleric, the truth!"

Aleric swallowed against the knot in his throat and forced the words out. "They tortured me until I pledged."

"There had to be another way!" Dartan protested, nearly shouting.

Aleric shook his head. He studied the scar across his open palm, avoiding the vampire's gaze. "There wasn't." He took a shuddering breath. "When you endure that level of pain...." The memories threatened to overwhelm him, images of blue fire, green steel, and the sound of breaking bones, his breaking bones. He shoved them back with a shake of his head. "They gave me no other way."

The silence that filled the room was charged with

Dartan's anger as he paced from one end to the other, his stride short and jerky compared to the vampire's usual grace. He finally paused near Aleric and faced him.

"They own you."

Aleric's lips pulled back in a snarl and he looked up at the vampire. "Nobody owns me," he said with a growl of frustrated rage.

Dartan held his heated gaze until the werewolf lowered his eyes. "I hoped it would be different here," Aleric admitted. "But the gorgons are looking for me. I'm a danger to everyone around me." He looked at Lilian. "You should go."

"I'm not leaving," she argued.

There was incomprehension on her face. She had no idea the level of danger Aleric's presence brought. He didn't know how to convey it to her.

Dartan sat back in his usual seat, but he didn't lean against the wall. His entire pose showed his discomfiture with all he had found out. He let out a breath. "Do I dare ask about the Horsemen?"

Aleric lifted a shoulder. "Considering the rest of what I had to do under the Drakathan's rule, the Horsemen were mild. We worked together at times. They knew I didn't enjoy what I was forced to do, and each of them was dictated by the limits set by their station. I suppose you could say we understood each other."

"Any chance you understood them enough to find Death?" the vampire asked.

Aleric shook his head. "Doyle's a bit of a loner, as you can imagine. If Wallace and Fabian don't know where to find him, that leaves me at a loss."

Dartan finally sat back. He studied the wall across from them. "So we're stuck."

Lilian leaned against Aleric's shoulder. "If only we could speak to the dead. I'm sure they know where to find him."

Her words tickled Aleric's thoughts. He looked at her. "What did you say?"

"I said, if only we could speak to the dead," she repeated, confused.

An idea struck the werewolf. "We might not be able to speak to the dead, but we can hallucinate about death. Or is it Death?"

"What are you talking about?" Dartan asked. He stared at Aleric as if he had sprouted a dozen arms.

"Dr. Worthen said he was sending the plague victims to the psychiatrist before they could be cleared to head home because many of them were hallucinating about death and dying." He pushed up to his feet. "I need to talk to the psychiatrist."

"Given your history, I agree," Dartan said, rising as well. "Perhaps you'll figure out why you did something so stupid as to pledge yourself to the Drakathan."

Aleric didn't answer. Both men held out a hand to Lilian. She looked from one to the other. Aleric and Dartan exchanged a glance, their hands still held out.

Lilian smiled and took Aleric's hand. He gave Dartan a triumphant grin as he helped her to her feet.

"Sorry, Dartan," Lilian said. "I hope you're not offended. It's just that—"

Dartan shook his head, his fangs revealed when he smiled. "You don't need to apologize." He put a hand on Aleric's shoulder as they walked. "It's about time someone chose this guy."

"About time?" Lilian repeated. "Haven't you only been here a few weeks?"

Dartan winked at her. "In the werewolf world, that's like

decades. They're a hopelessly romantic lot."

Aleric pushed open the doors to the D Wing and held them open.

"And vampires aren't?" he asked.

"Vampires are worse," Dartan admitted as the trio walked up the hallway. "If days without love for a werewolf feels like decades, for a vampire, the same span is centuries. We live on love. We thirst for it more than blood. We lie awake in our coffins pining over when the one we long after will proffer their figurative hearts. It's a curse."

Lilian chuckled at his melodramatic sigh. "I thought that since vampires live for so long, the days would feel short and insignificant, the memories in them trivial compared to the picture as a whole."

Dartan gave a single nod. "In lesser creatures, I suppose this is so. My theory is that vampires live so long because we are cold-hearted, our senses lessened, our ability to enjoy happiness or wallow in sadness stilted because of what we are. That is the reason for our long lives; we need the centuries to experience what humans and werewolves and others do in days." He gave her a long-suffering look. "It is the fate with which I've been gifted."

"So we shouldn't judge your womanizing ways?" Aleric asked.

Dartan's gaze lit up. "Exactly. It's merely my way of combining moments into the perfect tapestry of one single experience with enough magnitude to carry me through centuries of loneliness and bachelorhood when I grow old."

Lilian grinned. "You know I've heard college students say the exact same thing."

Dartan pushed the button for the elevator with a pensive look. "I should perhaps look into the college way of life."

The elevator beeped and the doors slid open.

Aleric followed the other two inside. "Those college girls don't stand a chance."

Dartan smiled. "You think they'd like the vampire type?"

"I have a feeling you'd be a hit there," Lilian replied. When the doors opened again, she led the way down the next hall. "You'd just have to figure out what to major in."

"Pre-med," Dartan and Aleric said at the same time.

Dartan chuckled. "Perhaps with a minor in blood analysis. I feel I'd have a head-start in that line of work."

"Except you're not supposed to drink the samples," Aleric pointed out.

"That's how I'd test them," Dartan replied.

Lilian paused by a door bearing the nametag 'Philomena Manors, Ph.D.'. She knocked.

"Come in," a woman's voice called out with a hint of an accent that ran the words together melodically.

Lilian pushed open the door.

"Lili, it's been forever!" a woman with long black hair exclaimed. She rose from her desk and crossed to Lilian. She and Lilian hugged before she stepped back to look at the men. After a brief glance over, she said, "You must be Dr. Wolf, and you're the resident vampire giving Nurse Tarli fits."

"I give her fits?" Dartan said in surprise.

"Everything gives her fits," Lilian replied.

"True," Philomena agreed. "But the fae definitely haven't helped. I'm still seeing the plague victims Dr. Worthen sends up here. We have a long road to travel yet."

"That's why we're here," Aleric told her. At the psychiatrist's curious look, he explained, "Dr. Worthen mentioned that the plague victims hallucinate about death and dying. I feel they may be the key to tracking down the Fourth Horseman and ending this plague for good."

Surprise showed on the woman's beautiful face. "Dr. Wolf, I believe you might be right. Have a seat."

She opened a drawer in her desk and pulled out a manila folder. "All of the plague victims have hallucinated to at least some extent, so on Dr. Worthen's recommendations, I've started a file on their accounts." She scanned through the pages. "Most are scattered and brief. After we discuss them, the patient is generally cleared to go home. Others, however," she flipped a few more pages, then pulled one out. "Like this one, are very clear and precise. I have these patients coming back for further evaluations to ensure that these visions don't interfere with their ability to live a normal life. Dr. Worthen's added your name to the approved physicians' list on the plague victims' files, so you can look at this."

She handed the folder to Aleric.

Aleric scanned the detailed description of a dark path, skeleton trees, a howling wind, and a house so dark just looking at it made the viewer afraid.

Yet the details weren't enough. He flipped through the pages, scanning each one. Aleric had hoped he could read the description and follow it to where Death was hiding out in the city. But the vague recollection of the plague victim's memories were sketchy. There was nothing Aleric could follow to find Doyle.

"I need to see it for myself."

Dartan made a sound of disbelief next to him. "What did you just say?"

Aleric looked up from the paper and met the gazes of his friends. "I can't follow this description to find Death. I need to get the plague; I need to see the hallucination for myself."

"You're not serious," Lilian protested.

"There's no way you're doing that," Dartan echoed.

Philomena shook her head. "I would highly suggested

against it, Dr. Wolf. From what I've seen, most of the plague victims recover to go on with their lives, but those who remember as well as this one will take months to clear from this hospital. It's not a safe course of action."

Aleric rose. "Just the same, I need to find Death as soon as possible. We've stopped the plague for now, but if he finds out it's no longer spreading, he'll go to other means. I need to find him and get to the bottom of his reasoning for interfering with the lives of humans in this city." His resolve solidified as he spoke. He looked at Dartan and Lilian. "I need some of those tomatoes."

"There's no way I'm helping with this," Dartan said firmly. "You're insane. Just ask the psychiatrist. She can diagnose you."

Aleric looked at Philomena.

She gave him a worried look. "Dr. Wolf, I don't think the course of action you want to take is a wise one. I've seen you put yourself at risk time and again." She reached into the drawer and pulled out another file. She handed it to him.

Chapter Thirteen

Aleric saw the name 'Dr. Aleric Bayne' written on the tab. He steeled himself and opened it. Inside were printed accounts of his battle with the demons, of him taking on the gargoyles, including a picture of him sprawled on his back on the Capitol Building steps, his eyes closed and the stone form of the gargoyle next to him. The caption read 'Dr. Wolf Sacrifices Self to Save Edge City.'

Aleric sat back down and set the folder on the psychiatrist's desk. He flipped further through the pages. There was a picture of him pinned to the ground by the silver stake through his shoulder, his gaze defiant and his teeth bared in a rictus of pain as he stared up at the Archdemon towering over him. The title 'Dr. Wolf Pits Self against Archdemon. Werewolf Prevails'.

"That doesn't look like I prevailed," Aleric noted, his voice soft. His shoulder gave a throb of pain in reply.

On sheets of yellow lined paper, in Philomena's elegant, swirled handwriting, were written accounts of the werewolf's actions inside and outside the hospital.

"Dr. Worthen worries you'll push yourself too far," the psychiatrist explained quietly. "It sounds like you've nearly been there a few times. I don't think getting the plague on purpose is a very sound decision, Doctor."

Aleric closed the folder and met her gaze. "Does letting Death continue to torment the humans of this city sound like a good course of action?" His words were quiet, calm. He had already made up his mind. "If I can make a difference here and protect others from getting hurt, I'll do it. I don't need anyone's approval."

He rose; the chair pushed back with a screech. He turned away, leaving his file on the desk.

"Aleric," Lilian said.

Aleric pulled the door open and walked back up the hallway. He heard Lilian hurrying after him. He reached the elevator and pressed the button. Lilian grabbed his arm.

"Aleric, look at me!"

He let out a slow breath and turned. "What?" he asked, his voice tight.

The look of compassion on Lilian's face was enough to take some of the frustration from him. She reached up a hand and pushed the dark hair back from his forehead that had become mussed by his abrupt actions.

"Aleric, talk to me."

He glanced up to see Dartan and Philomena standing in the doorway of her office. He knew his response had been rude, but he couldn't help himself.

"She had a whole file on me," he said quietly enough that his words couldn't be overheard. "You saw the others on her desk. Mine makes theirs look like poetry. My file was an entire tome."

She put a gentle hand on his arm. "Is that what's bothering you?"

"I'm not crazy," Aleric replied. There was a note of desperation in his voice. He wanted her to understand that his actions weren't those of a death-crazed psychopath. He wanted to help Edge City; he wanted to help his patients. If he had to put himself in the path of death or Death to do so, he wouldn't hesitate.

The elevator beeped and the doors slid open. Lilian's hand slipped into Aleric's. She stepped into the elevator and pulled him in after her. She pressed a button and the door shut. Aleric's last view of Dartan was of the vampire's arms crossed in front of his chest and a concerned expression on his face.

"I know you're not crazy," Lilian said. When Aleric didn't look at her, she put a hand on either side of his face and turned it gently so that he stared down at her. She rose on her tiptoes and kissed him softly, securely. When she stepped back, she said, "You're not crazy. Trust me."

Aleric put a hand to his lips. His heart pounded and his breath came short and stuttered. He stared at her. "Why did you do that?"

"You looked like you needed it," she replied.

The door slid open and she stepped out. When he didn't move, she held out a hand. "Come on. We need to go get Diablo and you have some things to tell me."

Aleric took her hand and allowed her to lead him down the hall. He could barely think past the whirl of emotions that filled his chest. His motions were automatic when he climbed into the car and sat in the passenger seat. Lilian pulled out of the parking lot.

"What do you want to know?" he asked.

"What does it mean to be pledged to those people in Blays?" Lilian glanced at him. "Dartan was pretty upset about that."

"He should be," Aleric replied. He looked out the window. It was one of the questions he wanted to avoid. Those were memories he never wanted to think about, things he had hidden away from when he found himself in Edge City. He let out a slow breath. "I told you the Drakathans gave me no choice. They captured me on purpose because they knew the nature of a werewolf would refuse to let me just give up and die. I have to keep fighting, even if that means enduring pain beyond belief, the inability to sleep, through lack of food, caged and solitary, alone with only my thoughts to torment me."

The memories were real again. Darkness pressed against him from every side. He closed his eyes and let them encompass his soul.

"I told you I was a beast when they found me, and that's true in every sense of the word. I had lost what made me a werewolf, what made me care about others, want to be in a pack, or fight for what I believed in. When the demons and vampires killed those I cared about, I lost my humanity. I think that's how they found me." He took a shuddering breath. "The Drakathans wanted me to refuse to pledge, because they delight in pain. When I refused, they tortured me until I couldn't remember what it meant to be a wolf, either. I became savage, uncontrollable. But that's what they wanted. They used their dark arts to keep me alive past what a normal werewolf could bear. They tortured me in ways people with even a shred of mercy wouldn't think of, and eventually, they broke me."

He fell silent. He felt the car stop, but kept his eyes closed. If he was going to tell her the truth, he wouldn't push the memories away until she knew everything. He needed to say it, to get it out and hope that in the end there was something left of him redeemable. If there was, Lilian would find it.

"When they broke me…." He paused, swallowed, and began again, "When they broke me, they brought a girl for the sacrifice."

"Sacrifice," Lilian said.

Aleric opened his eyes and looked at her. "Their pledge requires a sacrifice of life to bind the soul to them forever."

"How horrible!" she whispered with dread in her voice.

"It was," Aleric replied. He let the memory flow through him. "She was young, no more than fifteen or sixteen. She had golden hair that was tangled and unwashed from captivity with the Drakathan. There was terror in her eyes when she looked at me. She knew what was coming, and both of us understood that there was no way to get out of it."

Aleric closed his eyes again. He leaned his elbow on the door frame and tipped his face into his hand. "When they killed her, I just stood there. I knew what was coming. I knew there was no way out." Regret tightened his voice. "I stood there as they drew their blade across her throat and caught her lifeblood in a basket of marsh reeds. It was darker than I had thought it would be, swirling, with varying shades of red so deep I felt I could fall inside it and be lost forever." He closed his other hand into a fist and felt the answering throb of his shoulder. He welcomed the pain. "They poured her blood on me, binding me to them through her. I was their slave, their captive, for the rest of my life."

"But you're here," Lilian said, her voice soft.

"And so are the gorgons," Aleric replied. He lifted his head and looked at her. "They won't stop until they bring me back to do more unspeakable things for the Drakathans. They made me do so many horrible acts, bending me to their will and not caring if their whims ate away what was left of my soul." His voice quieted. "I passed my fill long ago, so I ran. I ran and I ran until I made it back to Drake City. I was running through the streets when I fell. I awoke at Edge City Hospital."

"So that's what you're doing there," Lilian said, her words filled with understanding.

"What?" Aleric asked, his voice haunted

"You're saving lives to atone for those you took. You're looking for redemption."

Aleric shook his head. He stared out the window. For the first time, he realized they were waiting in front of Dr. Worthen's house. He could see Diablo watching them out the window from her perch on the back of the couch Dartan had claimed. At his attention, the little winged kitten put a paw on the glass.

"There is no redemption for what I've done," Aleric said, his words bitter. "I deserve for the gorgons to find me. I should go back to the Drakathans and face my punishment. It's ridiculous to think I could make a difference here."

Lilian put a hand on Aleric's. "I'm alive because of you. You made a difference to me."

Aleric met her gaze. The depths of her bright blue eyes threatened to swallow him up. He wanted to stay there forever, to be the person he saw reflected in her gaze, the one she thought he was even though she had heard the darkness of his heart. The way she looked at him made him feel as though he had his humanity again, as if he was real and he mattered. It was a feeling he stored away in his mind in case it was ever taken from him. With her, he felt truly alive.

"Thank you," he told her, his words just above a whisper.

"I should be thanking you," she replied. She leaned over and kissed him.

Her lips caught him as much by surprise as the first time. He closed his eyes, tasting her, smelling her, being surrounded by all of her. It was a heady sensation and when she finally sat back, he felt dizzy and as if he could fly at the same time.

"Come on," she said. "Diablo doesn't understand why we're not going to get her."

She pushed open the car door, walked around, and took Aleric's hand as soon as he stepped out of the car. He followed her, caught in a swarm of mixed emotions from pouring out the darkest parts of his soul and soaring in one of the highest points of his life. Why she still walked next to him, smiling at him the way she did, was far beyond him.

He was a bad person, a dangerous man, someone whose presence should make others cross to the other side of the street, yet here she was, unlocking the door and beckoning him to follow her inside the house of her youth. One part of him whispered that he shouldn't follow her, that he should protect her by running away, that he should put as many miles between him and her as possible, yet the other part won. He stepped into the house and was met with her smile.

Diablo ran up with an accusatory meow. Aleric scooped her up and cuddled her, grateful for the distraction against the clashing emotions. Diablo wouldn't stop meowing and rubbing her face along Aleric's chin. He felt bad about leaving her for so long.

"I'll bring her some food and a bed," Lilian called over her shoulder. "Dad used to have an old tom cat named Fisher that lived with him here. I'm sure he still has some of Fisher's things."

"We're stopping by Perry's on the way back to the hospital, right?" Aleric asked.

There was a pause, then Lilian answered with a bit of reluctance, "Yes, we'll stop."

Perry was surprised to see them at such an early hour. Aleric wondered when the last time was that he had slept as he walked through the front door of Pasta-Pocalypse. The smell of pasta cooking, sauce boiling, and chopped tomatoes made him tired.

"You did it!" Perry exclaimed. The Horseman rushed out of the kitchen and hugged them both in his faintly glowing arms. "You fixed my restaurant! People have been coming from all over and there's not a sign of the plague. I love you both so much!" He kissed each of them on the cheek.

Aleric pushed away and wiped his cheek with his sleeve. "Great. Thanks. Glad to help a friend. Do you have any more of those plagued tomatoes left?"

Perry stared at him. "Why would I have any of those left?"

Aleric shrugged. "I don't know. In case of a rainy day, or just set aside by accident? Could you check?"

"I can," Perry replied. "But your request makes me uneasy. Could I perhaps interest you in some spaghetti instead?"

Aleric gave him a reassuring smile. "As fantastic as that sounds, we need to get back to the hospital. I'm working on locating Doyle, and I think the tomatoes might be the key."

"Ah," Perry said as if not at all surprised. "Good thinking. Hold on a sec."

Aleric petted Diablo and the kitten started to purr. He had put his sling back on under the pretense of wearing it so the minky had a place to sleep, but it eased the pressure of his shoulder enough that he wondered why he had taken it off in the first place. He refused to admit it to Lilian, but he had seen her look of understanding as she helped to adjust the straps. It bothered him that she was starting to know him so well.

Perry returned a few minutes later with a cardboard box. "I found this batch by the garbage can. I think the boys missed taking it out."

Aleric gave the box one sniff and nodded. "They're definitely plagued. Thanks, Perry." He crossed to the door, then paused. "Wallace says he and Fabian are going to return to Blays."

The news took the smile from the First Horseman's face. "Are they expecting me to go with them?"

Aleric shook his head. "Wallace agreed that you're better off here. He says it's about time you got to live your dreams."

The grin that filled Perry's face made it look as though it would split in two. "That's wonderful!" he exclaimed. He pushed open the door to the kitchen and called out, "Boys and girls, I'm sticking around!"

A cheer went up from the kitchen.

A hint of red brushed the Horseman's cheeks. "I guess they like working here," he said to Aleric and Lilian.

"I think they like their boss," Lilian replied.

The Horseman's answering smile stayed in Aleric's mind as he set the box of tomatoes in the trunk and sat back in the passenger seat. He knew eating a tainted tomato wasn't the smartest thing in the world to do, but if he couldn't find Death, who knew what the Fourth Horseman would be up to next. There was only one way to know for sure.

Aleric chose the Dark fae wing for his experiment. With Diablo on one knee and a tomato resting in his hand on the other, Aleric looked at his friends.

Dartan paced the room from one end to the other.

"This is ridiculous," he told the werewolf. "Remember what the psych said? Hallucinations of death and dying. You really don't have to go through with this."

"We both know that's not true," Aleric replied. He hoped he sounded calmer than he felt. His heart pounded in his chest and his tongue felt dry. The last thing he wanted to do was to place the tomato in his mouth. Tomatoes had never been his favorite fruit; after this, he doubted he would ever eat another one.

"Are you sure there's not another way?" Lilian asked again. She waited on a chair next to the bed on which Aleric sat. Her expression was uncertain. "Maybe I should ask Dad to be here."

"No!" Aleric said.

"Don't do it," Dartan echoed.

Aleric gave the vampire a curious look. "Why don't you want Dr. Worthen in here?"

Dartan crossed his arms defensively. "He may or may not know about the box of blood bags I borrowed." He gestured to the small, portable refrigerator box in the corner. "I figured it wouldn't hurt to keep some on hand."

"I think that's a good idea," Lilian replied. "I really don't think he'd mind."

She was watching the vampire as he paced to the back of the room. Both of them were looking away. Aleric felt it was as good a time as any to avoid being stopped. He put the tomato to his mouth. The taste of sulfur filled his mouth when he bit down.

"I don't want to be forced to lie," Dartan continued, "But

that nurse, Talia, asks a lot of questions and— Aleric!"

He reached the werewolf's side with the speed of a raging vampire, but Aleric had already swallowed the bite. It left a bitter aftertaste in his mouth.

"You shouldn't have done that," the vampire breathed.

"I'm the only one who should have," Aleric replied.

"Spit it out," Dartan demanded.

"I swallowed it."

"I'm sure you have a gag reflex," Dartan pointed out. "I once heard of a werewolf who gagged every time he ate vegetables. Maybe that'll work on you. Werewolves are more of a meat and more meat type. I doubt vegetables are good for you even if they aren't plagued. You should gag it up just on principle."

"Tomatoes aren't vegetables," Lilian said with her attention on Aleric.

"Well that's ridiculous," Dartan shot back. "Next thing I know, you're going to tell me they're a fruit."

"They are," Lilian replied.

Aleric felt sick to his stomach. The sensation abruptly changed to one of need. As if of its own accord, his hand lifted the tomato to his mouth once more.

Dartan snatched the fruit away before he could bite it again. "I think you've had enough," the vampire said.

Lilian touched Aleric's knee. "How do you feel?"

"Strange," Aleric replied. His voice echoed in his mind. He looked around the room. His vision was blurry; he blinked, but it refused to clear up.

"Look at his eyes," Dartan whispered.

Diablo hissed. Aleric felt more than saw Lilian pick up the minky and try to sooth her. He knew without glancing in a mirror that his eyes had turned the white of the plague victims'. He felt lethargic and numb, and above all, very hungry. He wanted to fight the vampire, to do anything in his power to get the tomato back and eat the entire thing. His mouth watered at the thought. It was all he could do to remain sitting.

"Is the I.V. ready?" Dartan asked. Aleric could hear the worry in the vampire's voice through the strange hum that filled his ears.

"Ready to go," Lilian replied.

"Alright." Dartan turned to Aleric. "Do you see anything?"

Aleric shook his head. The movement made the humming sound increase. He could taste the purple drool that filled his mouth. He wanted to spit it out, but kept from acting on the impulse. The less he grossed out Lilian, the better he felt it would be for their relationship.

"I-I think I'm going to lay down," he said.

His friends eased him back onto the bed with gentle hands.

Aleric closed his eyes.

Darkness filled his mind. As exhausted as he had been, he knew he wasn't asleep by the way the hallucination felt.

He was walking down the street. His footsteps echoed strangely in his mind. One step, one echo. Another step, another echo. The echoes changed to two and he knew he wasn't alone. He glanced back, but nobody was there.

"Where are you?" he called.

Somewhere else, in some place far away from where he stood, he heard Lilian say, "He's moaning. Is he in pain? Should I give him the I.V.?"

"Wait," Dartan directed, his voice tight. "He has to find it, or this is all a worthless risk."

Aleric continued down the street. Mist swirled, creating shapes that almost became people before they vanished away.

He peered into alleys that were so dark in their depths that he knew nothing could exist there.

He felt the direction he should go. Faces became apparent in the darkness. Features grew more distinct. They were victims of the Drakathans, fae creatures he had helped to gather and place at the Drakathans' merciless doorstep. They haunted his path, reaching for him with hands he could not feel. Their eyes were accusing, their mouths twisted in the pain of their torture at the hands of his captors.

Death was everywhere. The plague victims were right. Aleric felt tears running down his cheeks. He wanted to go back, to pretend like none of it had happened. He wished he could forget about his past; yet everywhere he looked, it haunted him.

"Look at his tears; he's in pain," Lilian said, her words thick with compassion. "I need to start the I.V." Her voice echoed through the darkness, creating something for Aleric to hang onto.

"I don't think it's that kind of pain," Dartan replied, his words heavy. A hand touched Aleric's shoulder. He felt it through the space between them. "Hang in there, Wolfie. You can do this."

Aleric pulled in a breath that smelled of sulfur. He continued forward. The souls pressed around him from every side until he could no longer move.

"I have you to thank for these, Aleric Bayne."

The voice echoed all around him, its tone a deep, rolling bass that was both accusatory and mocking.

"I know," Aleric replied. He searched the mist, hoping to locate the source of the words. "I have done horrible things."

"You try to change that now?" There was a note of humor to Death's voice.

"I know I can't change the past," Aleric replied. "I just

want to make the present better."

"How do you intend to do that?" There was a tone to the Fourth Horseman's words that said he guessed what the werewolf was going to say.

"I want you to return Fluffy to Fabian and leave Blays with your brothers," Aleric told him.

The voice fell silent for a moment. Doyle cleared his throat. "I can't."

"Because of Haga," Aleric said, remembering.

"Yes," Doyle replied with surprise in his voice. "Where did you hear that?"

"From Wallace."

The Horseman gave a huff. "You do get around."

"You've left me no choice," Aleric replied. "You're affecting my city."

"Indirectly," Doyle told him. "Humans are frail things in some ways, stronger in others. They're interesting."

"They also deserve to live their own lives without being tormented by the Four Horsemen. You belong in Blays."

"I won't return without Haga. Why else do you think I did all of this? I knew you would find her."

Death's words caught Aleric off-guard. "You mean you knew I would come after you in this way?"

Death chuckled. The sound made the mist whirl around Aleric. He felt the fingers of his victims brushing his arms, back, and chest.

"You're the fae hero of this human city, Dr. Wolf. I've heard your name whispered in the streets, your legend told in the shadows. You've created quite the impact since you awoke here." The Horseman's voice lowered. "I knew if anyone could find Haga, you would be the one. I also knew if I involved the humans you seem to care about so much, you'd come running without hesitation. Your bravery is about as commendable as your death wish; trust me when I say I know what I'm talking about."

"I'll find Haga," Aleric promised. "Send your brothers back to Blays and I'll do anything I need to keep this city safe."

"I knew you would do it," Doyle said. "You have an antiquated sense of honor lost among most."

The victims in the mist grew stronger. They grabbed at Aleric's arms, pulling him from side to side with bruising grips. He could feel their hands raking down his back, dragging at his feet, trying to draw him down.

"Tell me how to find her," Aleric said. There was a note of desperation in his voice. If they got too strong before he was finished speaking to Death, he wondered if he would be able to break free.

"She was being chase by your beloved friends," Death said, his voice dry. "The Drakathans thought if they could capture her, they would have power over me. They chased her through the Rift. When I heard she was in danger, I asked my brothers to come along to help. I found blood; I fear she was wounded by gorgons."

Aleric realized who the Horseman was talking about. He struggled to keep his footing. "Is she a woodland elf?"

"Yes!" Death replied. "Do you know where she is?"

"I do," Aleric told him. "She was bitten by gorgons. I gave her the antidote. We're waiting to see if she recovers."

Death was silent for a moment. "She's not in my realm," he said finally. "She must still be alive." There was hope in the Horseman's voice.

"She was when I left the hospital." The fingers tightened. Claws scratched down Aleric's back and chest. "I need to get out of here to bring her to you!" he called as the mass pressed tighter around him.

"I'll find you," Doyle replied, his voice fading beneath the rising cries of the fray that surrounded Aleric. "You must pay for your actions. You must answer to them for your crimes."

The mass climbed over Aleric, pressing him to the ground beneath hands and feet that punched and raked, clawed and pulled. He cried out at the pain of fingers driving into his shoulder where the silver stake had gone. He gasped at hands pressing into his eyes and feet kicking his head.

Aleric tried to suck in a breath, but he couldn't past the weight of bodies on his chest. He struggled, but hands held him down. He opened his mouth to yell, but fingers slid inside, blocking his air. Anger, helplessness, frustration, and fear pressed in from every side. He closed his eyes and gave himself over to the onslaught he knew he deserved.

Chapter Fourteen

"Let me go!" Aleric shouted.

"Whoa, Wolfie! Hold still!"

Aleric's eyes flew open at the sound of Dartan's voice. He looked around wildly, expecting to see the faces in the mist leering down at him with accusations in their eyes, their voiceless mouths opened in snarls of anger.

"It's okay," Lilian said. "We've got you." She held his elbow where the I.V. ran. Aleric could feel the life-saving fluid flowing through his veins.

The werewolf's heart pounded so loud he was amazed it

didn't burst through his chest. Aleric lifted his left arm to look for the marks from the victims, but there were none. The only pain he felt was in his shoulder; for the moment, the ache was actually a relief.

Diablo stood on his chest. The little minky meowed and rubbed her head against his face. He let out a relieved breath and petted the winged kitten softly.

"That must have been some dream," Dartan said.

Aleric shook his head. "It wasn't a dream." He tried to sit up.

Dartan put a hand on the werewolf's chest, holding him down as though he was as weak as the kitten.

"Easy, Aleric. Slow down. You need a break after that," the vampire told him.

"I need to find Death," Aleric replied. He tried to push the vampire's hand away, but Dartan didn't move or give any sign that he put effort into holding the werewolf down. It was infuriating.

"You almost found him," Dartan said. "I think you need to reevaluate your position here."

That caught Aleric's attention. "What do you mean?"

"I mean that if you keep putting yourself in harm's way like this, Death is going to find you a whole lot sooner."

"He's right."

Aleric looked at Lilian. There were shadows under her eyes. He realized with a start that she had gone without sleep to stay at his side.

"If you keep pushing yourself like this, you're going to crash," she told him. There was sympathy in her tired gaze. "Aleric, I don't know how much longer you're going to be able to keep going. We need you here. If you don't take care of yourself, someone will do it for you."

A small half-smile lifted the corner of Aleric's mouth.

"You're going to take care of me?"

She nodded. "Someone has to. You can't expect Dartan to be the only one who cares whether you drop dead from exhaustion or whatever else you put yourself through. You have a family here who cares about you."

"Yeah," Dartan agreed. "Tell you what. If you don't lay there until the rest of that I.V. goes through, I'm getting Nurse Eastwick and Dr. Worthen. They'll have a thing or two to say about your condition."

Aleric stopped pushing against the vampire's hand, as futile as the action was. He let his head fall back against the pillow on the bed. Diablo celebrated by curling up beneath his chin. The purr that rumbled from her tiny body was loud enough to make everyone smile.

"I think she agrees with you," Aleric admitted.

"We all need a rest," Lilian said. "I'm going to go take a nap in the breakroom. Promise me you'll stay here until I return."

Aleric knew he could leave while she was gone, but if she needed to trust him to rest, he wouldn't break that. "I promise," he said. "Go get some sleep. You need it."

She leaned down and kissed him on the forehead. "You need it, you stubborn werewolf."

Aleric's eyelids threatened to close of their own accord. He had to admit how exhausted he felt. The brief stint with the plague had taken a lot from him, but there was one more thing he had to do.

"Dartan, could you check on the woodland elf for me? I need to know if the antidote worked." He paused, then said, "She's the one Death's been looking for."

Dartan's shock would have been hilarious if the fate of Edge City didn't rest on the elf's shoulders. "I'll check right away. How do we get her back to him?"

"He said he'll come to me. He knows where we are." Aleric was too tired to decide whether that was a good thing or bad. "The sun's up. I'll take her out to him when he gets here."

"When you wake up," Dartan said, his tone stern.

Aleric nodded. "When I wake up."

He awoke to the feeling of Lilian's fingers brushing his hair off his forehead. The I.V. had been removed from his arm, its tube looped next to the empty bag on the pole.

"Haga's awake," she said. "The Horsemen are in the back parking lot. They asked me to come get you."

Aleric sat up and was glad to find his strength had returned.

"How long did I sleep?" he asked.

"A few hours," she replied. "It's noon."

He pushed off the bed and was happy to find his head clear and strength back.

"How are you feeling?" Lilian asked.

"Much better," Aleric replied. "Who knew sleep could be so good for a person?" He rubbed his shoulder. Even it was feeling a bit better.

Lilian laughed as she led the way to the door. "I could have told you that."

"I'm going to have to listen to you more often," Aleric said.

He pushed open the door to the D Wing and stared at the mass of hospital staff members crowding the hallway. Necks were craning and people rose on tiptoes to get a glimpse of the Horsemen out the back door. A glance toward the door showed Dr. Worthen waiting halfway down the hall, his stern expression keeping the staff at bay.

"It's about time," the head physician said when Aleric met his gaze. "You have some serious explaining to do."

Aleric crossed to him with a wry smile. "You'll get the whole story," he promised. "But for now, I hear it's not polite to keep the Horsemen waiting. Nobody wants to start an Apocalypse."

He and Lilian exchanged a look. He fought back a smile.

They found Dartan waiting with the woodland elf near the backdoor.

The elf surprised Aleric by giving him a weak hug. "Thank you, Dr. Wolf, for your care. They told me about the antidote and the plague. You're a brave man."

Aleric felt embarrassed at the praise. "I'm glad you're going home."

"Me, too," she replied. "I've missed Doyle. I hear he made a bit of a ruckus trying to find me."

"A bit," Aleric agreed, smiling at the understatement. "He certainly cares about you."

Dartan ducked away from the sunlight when Aleric opened the back door. He helped Haga outside into the healing light. He was relieved to see three of the four Horsemen standing in the parking lot. They made quite an ominous sight standing by their steeds in the bright light of day.

"You forgot this," Dartan called from behind him.

Aleric turned to see the vampire throw something. He caught the object and opened his hand to reveal the small salamander totem on his palm.

"I'll bring it back to you," he promised.

"Just make sure you come back," Dartan replied before he shut the door.

"I'm going to miss you so much!" Lilian said.

Aleric turned to see her kneeling in front of the two grims. The children stood next to Fabian. Each held the blankets and treasures Lilian and the werewolf had given the grim children.

"Fabian promised us real beds and a chance to go to school," Grimsli said.

"Yeah," Grimma pipped up, her voice excited. "And he said we can ride Fluffy whenever we want."

The Second Horseman patted the black horse on the nose. "I'm just happy to have him back."

"I'm sorry I took him from you. I had to ensure that the werewolf would find me."

Aleric followed the voice to the Fourth Horseman. He stood near the garbage cans with a scythe in one hand. Behind him, a horse that glowed greenish-yellow and had red eyes sniffed at the contents of the metal garbage containers.

"Doyle!" the woodland elf said.

At the sight of her, the Horseman dropped his scythe and his horse's reins and ran to her. His black cloak billowed behind him in a mass of shadows that rose and fell with the movement. The tall, pale Horseman scooped her up gently in his arms and hugged her the way one hugs a fragile person in fear of injuring them.

"Are you alright, sweetheart?" he asked.

"I am now," she replied. "I'm ready to go home."

"Me, too," he said. He met Aleric's gaze over the woodland elf's shoulder. "Thank you. The plague is gone completely. You'll find that the victims have also lost all recollection of their hallucinations. I promised Perry that his crops will be pestilence free from now on."

"Thank you," Aleric replied. "I appreciate your help."

The Horseman nodded. "So how do we get back to Blays?"

Aleric held up the salamander totem. The confused looks on the Horsemen's faces made him smile as he led the way through the alleys toward the Rift.

"This isn't going to hurt, is it?" Wallace asked. He eyed the open Rift with uncertainty.

"It looks like fun to me," Grimma said. She ran through with Grimsli close behind.

"Leave it to children to teach us what courage means," Fabian said with a smile. He grinned at Aleric. "Here's to hoping you never have to deal with us again."

He urged his horse through with a click of his tongue and disappeared after the grims.

"If Fabian can do it, I can do it," Wallace said. He gave Aleric an embarrassed look. "I am War, after all. I'm supposed to be the tough one. I can't believe I let children go before me."

"Take care of yourself," Aleric told the Horseman. "Enjoy the border wars."

"I always do," Wallace replied. He urged his blood-red horse through.

Doyle and Haga looked down at Aleric from atop Death's glowing pale horse.

"I've heard whispers of your name a few times," Doyle said. "I thought I would see you in my realm before now."

"I'm trying to avoid it as long as I can," Aleric replied.

Doyle gave a grim smile. "Not a bad idea." Haga set a hand on the Fourth Horseman's arm and whispered something in his ear. He sat back with a nod. "Haga reminds me that I have something for you. A gift."

"A gift for me?" Aleric replied in uncertainty. He wasn't sure he wanted a gift from the Horseman of Death.

Doyle put his hand inside his black cloak. When he withdrew it, he held a glowing green orb. "Death doesn't take you from yourself," he said, his deep voice echoing off the walls despite the quietness of his words. "Death reveals you to yourself, and what better way to know who you are than through the memory of others."

Aleric reached up a hand to the orb. The moment he touched it, warmth ran through him as though hot water had been poured on him from head to toe. He closed his eyes and the memory rushed into his thoughts.

"That's my little boy."

Aleric found that he was watching a version of himself far younger than his memories ran.

"You're so smart, aren't you?"

The voice was his father's. Aleric looked up from his vantage point behind the little boy who couldn't have been more than two years old.

"You figured it out, didn't you?"

The man who watched him appeared younger than Aleric remembered. His brown hair had not yet been touched with gray and his eyes crinkled at the corners with his smile instead of disapproval.

His father bent down, picked up the sticks, and tossed them again.

All at once, Aleric remembered the game. His father had made the sticks, choosing them one by one from the forest near their house. He had whittled them for days, smoothing the bark away and carving small pictures into their ends. He had then taken ash from the fireplace and rubbed it into his carvings so that they stood out stark against the pale wood.

Aleric remembered pushing himself, seeing how quickly he could place bear to bear, turtle to turtle, pixie to pixie until the sticks created a circle. The delighted smile on his father's face filled him with such happiness.

"That's my boy," his dad said. "That's my little Ricky. I'm so proud of you."

The memory faded.

"I had forgotten," Aleric said. He wiped at the tears on

his cheeks as he looked up at Death and the woodland elf the Horseman loved. "I had completely forgotten."

"I know," Doyle said, his voice carrying understanding. "He wanted you to know."

Aleric's voice was thick when he asked, "Does that mean my father's with you?"

The Horseman lowered his head in one noble nod. "He is."

The knowledge made Aleric's throat tighten. "Take good care of him, will you?"

Doyle smiled. "I always do. Death is not a thing to fear, Aleric Bayne." His gaze sharpened. "But it is also not a thing to go searching for. If I have to come back for you far sooner than I intend, I will be disappointed. This is your second chance. Don't throw it away."

"I won't," Aleric replied. "I promise."

He watched the Fourth Horseman cross through the Rift. After he passed, the hole closed and the view of the Glass District was swallowed up into the dark alley once more. Aleric caught the salamander totem and put it in his pocket. He leaned against the wall and closed his eyes, letting the memory run over him once more.

Chapter Fifteen

Lilian was gone when Aleric returned. He found Dr. Worthen and Dartan sitting in the break room.

"So the sphinx went home?" Dr. Worthen asked when Aleric took a seat on the couch near him.

Diablo flapped her wings and landed on the werewolf's knee. Aleric petted her and she gave a contented purr. "Yep. Everyone made it back safely. Even the grims. I'm sad to see them go, but I'm glad they found a better home," Aleric replied.

"Anywhere is better than living in an alley," Dartan said.

"Not anywhere," Aleric told him. "Some alleys have their charm."

Dr. Worthen gave him a relieved smile. "The plague victims are gone, the D wing is empty, and everyone's safe. You did a good job."

"Something still bothers me, though," Aleric said.

"What's that?" Dartan asked.

Aleric was about to reply when Gregory walked into the room. The orderly grinned at the sight of Aleric. "Did you tell him, Doc?"

"I thought I'd leave it to you," Dr. Worthen said.

"Tell me what?" Aleric asked.

"I want you to help me propose to Therese. You gave so much money to my ring fund that it would only be fair." Gregory said the words so quickly the werewolf could barely follow them. "I know you care about our relationship and it would only be fitting that you help because you've been such a great supporter. There's this bridge and I think it would be perfect because Therese loves bridges. Would you help?"

Aleric was amazed the man had said the entire thing without taking a breath. He waited for the meaning of the words to sink in.

"Say 'yes', Wolfie," Dartan whispered.

"Uh, yes," Aleric replied. He was a bit uncertain if he had agreed to help the orderly propose or build a bridge.

"Thank you, Doc!" Gregory said. He threw his arms around Aleric as if he couldn't help himself and gave the werewolf a hug. "There's so much to get ready! So where do we start?"

Out of the corner of his eye, Aleric saw Dr. Worthen and Dartan stand and head for the door.

"Where do we start what?" Aleric asked.

"The proposal! I don't know what to say."

Aleric stared at the orderly. "I've never proposed to anyone before."

"But you're good with words," Gregory pointed out. "I saw you on the television. You always seem to know exactly what to say." He let out a sound of desperation. "I don't know what to say. From what I've seen on television, a proposal has to be perfect! I can't mess this up or it will ruin my life forever. You've got to help me, Dr. Wolf, you've just go to!"

"Catch you later," Dartan said with a grin.

"Yes, good luck," Dr. Worthen told Aleric before he followed the vampire out the door. Aleric heard the head physician chuckle when he reached the hallway.

The werewolf turned back to find that Gregory had procured a pen and a torn piece of paper from somewhere. The orderly waited with an expectant gaze. Aleric sat up straight and searched his mind for anything that could help with the situation. He also made a mental note to thank Dartan for throwing him under the proverbial griffin. He wondered what creatures he could fill the Dark fae wing with next.

***

That evening found all of them at the Edge City North Park. Aleric tugged at the neck of the suit he wore.

"It's a tuxedo. It's supposed to be uncomfortable," Dr. Worthen said from Aleric's left side. He tugged at his own collar. "I swear the rented ones are the worst."

"Quiet," Nurse Tarli shushed them. "They'll be here soon." She glared at Aleric. "Try not to ruin this."

Aleric wanted to point out that he hadn't ruined anything as far as he could recall, but he knew arguing with the nurse was pointless. He turned his attention to their surroundings.

Lilian, Nurse Eastwick, and Nurse Tarli had lit candles along the entire bridge. The reflection of the flames in the water of the wide river below was captivating. White rose petals had been strewn along the walkway of the bridge, and each of them wore matching roses in their tuxedo lapels and in the girls' hair. Aleric had found his eyes straying to Lilian frequently as they waited for the couple to arrive. She met his gaze and held it. There was a look in her eyes as though she knew just how captivating she appeared in her flowing blue dress that set off her eyes just the right way.

"They're here!" Dartan exclaimed, tearing Aleric's attention back to the matter at hand.

"Everyone be calm," Dr. Indley said. The veterinarian's face beamed as she stood at the vampire's side.

Nurse Eastwick couldn't contain an exclamation of, "They look so adorable!"

"What's all this?" Aleric heard Therese ask as Gregory helped her from the car.

"Oh, this?" he said in a forced nonchalant tone. "Really nothing. It's nothing. Nothing at all." He looped her arm through his. "Allow me to lead you forward."

"I don't really believe this is nothing," Therese said, her eyes wide and a confused look on her face as she walked beside him. "It most definitely looks like something."

"Trust me, darling," Gregory said.

He led her past his waiting colleagues to the middle of the bridge. To Therese's shock, he then lowered to one knee and pulled a small black box from his jacket pocket.

"Therese Angela Varney, I've asked our friends to gather here to witness the profession of my love for you."

Therese's hand flew to her mouth.

"Therese, you are everything that makes my life beautiful." Aleric mouthed the words he had helped the orderly write. "You are my sun, my moon, and my stars. You are the light of my life, my joy, my every happiness, and I can't imagine spending another day without you by my side."

A smile filled Aleric's face. He had given a few suggestions, then asked the orderly how he felt about the girl he wanted to marry. It had only taken some gentle steering to keep Gregory on the right path.

"I feel as though I have always known you, that you have always been with me, helping me to this moment so that I can ask you to be my wife and never part from me again." He opened the box and Therese gasp at the beautiful ring inside. "Therese, without you, I cannot breathe, I cannot smile, I cannot live. I would follow you to the ends of the earth and back just to be near you. Please say that you'll be my wife so that I can always have the most beautiful thing in the world at my side."

"Oh, Greggie," Therese said. Tears had filled her eyes, making them shine in the light of the moon and candles. "I would love to be your wife."

"So yes?" Gregory asked.

"Yes, yes, a million times yes!" Therese replied. She

dropped to her knees and hugged him as sobs shook her shoulders.

"Why are you crying?" Gregory asked in alarm.

"These are happy tears," Therese replied.

The hospital staff smiled at each other. Aleric couldn't help comparing the way Lilian's eyes sparkled compared to the beauty of the flames dancing on the water. He looked down at the candlelight and froze.

"There's a person in the river," he said.

"What?" Dartan asked.

"Someone's in the river!" Aleric repeated.

He ran to the edge of the bridge and vaulted over the side. He heard the shouts and calls of surprise from his friends before he dove beneath the surface.

Aleric realized diving into a river when he had no idea of the depth or if there were rocks along the bottom was a stupid thing to do. Fortunately, the darkness swallowed him up without dashing his brains out on a boulder hidden beneath the surface. He floundered for a second as he debated which way was up. A glance over his head showed the light of the moon. He breathed a sigh of relief for the object that had saved his life on more than once occasion and kicked toward the top.

"Where is he?" Nurse Eastwick called as soon as his head surfaced.

"I see him!" Dartan replied.

"Thank goodness," Lilian said.

Aleric swam toward the body that had caught his attention. It floated on its side in the water. Aleric grabbed a foot and paused at the feeling of a hoof in his hand. He pulled and the body turned. Aleric stared at the still face of the faun Braum he had helped return to health and then back to Blays not long before.

Aleric hooked an arm over the faun's chest and beneath his arm. He swam for shore where the entire proposal crowd gathered and was cheering him on. Aleric's shoulder threatened to give out. His good one held onto the faun which put the strain on his left arm as he pulled them through the water.

"I've got him."

Dartan reached Aleric and grabbed the faun from the werewolf. Together, they swam to the shore and the waiting crowd.

"He's not breathing," Lilian said.

"I'm starting CPR," Nurse Eastwick replied. "Call the ambulance."

After a few tense minutes of chest compressions, the faun responded by coughing up water. The nursing staff quickly rolled Braum onto his side. The ambulance pulled up near the edge of the river. The EMTs rushed down and worked on Braum without hesitating at his fae form.

Aleric and Dr. Worthen rode in the ambulance back to the hospital.

"That was quick thinking back there," the doctor said. "You may have saved his life."

"I'll feel better when he wakes up," Aleric replied.

"Me, too," Dr. Worthen agreed.

Though the nurse's administrations followed by the EMTs' quick work had gotten the faun breathing again, his heartbeat was weak and his breaths were shallow. Aleric couldn't help feeling responsible for the faun's condition. He had no idea why Braum would have gone into the river. Fauns didn't swim as a rule. He must have been desperate.

"He's stable," Dr. Worthen told Aleric later after reviewing the faun's examination reports. "We'll watch the monitors and hope for signs of improvement. Only time will tell."

Aleric brought the faun to the Light fae side of the D Wing. He positioned Braum's bed beneath the window that would catch the most sun when the night gave way to day. It never failed to remind him of the fairy Tranquility who had practically turned the D Wing upside-down in her need to take care of everything on the Light fae side and make it perfect. He took a seat, grateful for the friends he had found in Edge City.

"I'm sorry about Braum," Lilian said. She stood behind Aleric with a hand on his shoulder. "The nurses say he's a very nice guy."

"He is," Aleric agreed. "I just wish I knew how he ended up in the river. He was happy to go back to Blays." He fell silent again.

"Is there anything you'd like me to bring you while you wait?" she asked.

Aleric gave her a grateful smile. "No, thank you. I think I'll just keep an eye on him for a while. It couldn't hurt."

"It couldn't," she agreed. "He'd be glad to know he has a friend watching over him." When it was clear the werewolf was prepared to spend the rest of the night in vigil at Braum's side, Lilian rose. "I'm going to talk with Vallia."

"Alright," Aleric replied, his attention on the faun.

Diablo pattered up to him and climbed up his pant leg. She settled on his knee. When he ran his fingers through her soft fur, a purr emanated from her chest. The sound never failed to bring a smile to Aleric's face. He leaned back in the chair and let his thoughts wander in time to the steady beeping of the monitor near Braum's head.

A few hours later, Aleric heard familiar footsteps enter the room. A quiet hiss said the UV lights were still doing their job.

"I forgot to ask why you put the lights back up," Aleric said with a glance back at his friend. "It seems a bit inconvenient for you."

"For the fun of it," the vampire replied. He ran a hand over his face with a grimace.

"Looks like a blast," Aleric said dryly at the sight of the sunburn on the vampire's skin from the lights.

Dartan pulled up a chair beside the werewolf. "Honestly?" he said. "Remember that day there was blood all over the E.R. from the patient who slit his wrists?"

Aleric nodded.

Dartan let out a breath. "It set me off. I was blood-crazy and I couldn't think. I wanted to break you in two."

"I remember," Aleric replied quietly.

Dartan waved his elegant fingers toward the UV lights. "I put those there to help me snap out of it if that ever happens while I'm in the D Wing. I can put up with a little pain, but the thought of killing someone innocent haunts me."

Aleric nodded. "Putting up with a little discomfort to help others live. That's honorable."

Dartan gestured to Aleric's shoulder. The werewolf hadn't realized he was rubbing it again. "You know what you're talking about," the vampire said.

Aleric dropped his hand. "It bothers me a bit."

"Why do I feel like that's an understatement?" Dartan asked.

Silence fell between them. It was comfortable and without tension as the two friends from far difference circumstances watched the motionless form of the faun on the bed.

"No change?" Dartan asked.

"None," the werewolf replied.

Dartan crossed his arms and leaned back in his chair.

"What was it that was bothering you?"

Aleric focused on the vampire. "What are you talking about?"

"When we were in the break room before Gregory asked your help with the proposal." A toothy grin spread across his face. "Good job by the way."

Aleric gave the vampire a mocking glare. "You set me up."

"Werewolves are hopeless romantics, remember?" Dartan replied. "You were made for proposals and all that mushy stuff."

"What about your 'each day is like a century apart from love for a vampire' lecture?" Aleric reminded him.

"That's beside the point," the vampire said. "Back to the topic at hand. You said something still bothered you."

Aleric ran a hand across the minky's wings. "The gorgons. That's what's bothering me. Why haven't they come back? If they were supposed to bring me to the Drakathans, they should have been here by now. The Four Horsemen knew where to find me, so why not the gorgons?"

"You've been waiting for them to attack all this time?" Dartan said, his eyebrows pulled together in surprise. "That'll make a person tense."

Aleric nodded. "But they haven't. It's like the gorgons have forgotten about me. I'm not complaining, but how do we find them and get them out of the city if they aren't on my trail?"

"They d-don't want you."

Aleric and Dartan stared down at the faun.

Braum's eyes were open, his face pale.

"Braum! You're awake!" Aleric exclaimed. "What happened?"

"Important," the faun said, his words weak. "Came to wwarn you."

"Warn me?" Aleric repeated. "Warn me about what? What's worth coming all the way back here for?"

"The egg. A-almedragon."

Cold rushed through Aleric so fast he was amazed his breath didn't fog. He stood, staring from the faun to Dartan with such horror on his face that the vampire pushed up from his own chair.

"What is it?" Dartan demanded.

"The gorgons aren't after me," Aleric said with shock in his voice. "They're after her."

"Who?" Dartan asked, his words colored with exasperation.

"The vampiress, Vallia," Aleric replied. "They want her blood to create a dragon in Edge City."

Dartan shook his head. "There's no way."

Aleric was already running to the door.

The vampire fell in easily beside him. "So there's a dragon in the city. Big deal. You've sent gargoyles and demons home. What's a creature the size of a horse scaring you so badly? You've got to explain this to me, Wolfie."

Aleric shoved through the doors to the Emergency Room. He spotted Gregory and Nurse Eastwick sorting through supplies.

"Gregory, can I borrow your car?" he asked.

"You can have anything you want. The proposal was perfect!" the orderly exclaimed. He tossed his keys and Aleric caught them. He held out Diablo for Gregory to take. The orderly accepted the minky and cuddled her close.

"Don't worry, I love cats," he said.

The werewolf turned to the nurse. "Nurse Eastwick, Braum's awake. Can you see to his needs while I'm gone?"

"I'm on my way," the nurse replied.

Aleric ran back down the hallway with Dartan close behind.

"Aleric, really!" the vampire said.

Aleric paused near the door. His heart pounded so loud he was amazed the vampire didn't comment on it.

"Regular dragons are born to grow the size of horses. They're docile; they keep to themselves. But the Drakathan found that a dragon hatched in a certain type of blood became something far greater than that. I only saw one once, and that was enough. It could breathe fire, claw through brick, and soar from the skies with enough force to level a building when it landed. The Almedragon will destroy Edge City."

"You said a certain type of blood," Dartan repeated.

Aleric nodded. "The only time I saw an Almedragon, a vampiress was sacrificed for it to hatch."

"Vallia," the vampire breathed. His eyes widened. "What are we waiting for?"

They both rushed out into the night. Aleric forgot all about traffic laws as he raced through the streets of Edge City. He pulled up to the subway entrance in a screech of tires.

"Drive like that again and I'll tell Gregory to never let you borrow his car again," Dartan threatened.

"It's still in one piece," Aleric said as he ran down the stairs after the vampire.

"Well I'm not," Dartan said over his shoulder. "I'm going to have to see that cute psychiatrist at the hospital to get over your driving."

"It's not that bad," Aleric shot back as they ran into the subway tunnel. "If you need to an excuse to go flirt with her, you'd better come up with something better than that."

Dartan pulled on the hidden ribbon and the door opened.

They tore down the stairs.

"She'll be here," Dartan said.

"She's got to be here," Aleric seconded.

They both pushed on the wooden door. It swung inward and hit the wall with a bang. Aleric and Dartan stopped.

The delicate, beautifully decorated interior of the vampiress' lair had been torn to pieces. The fine couches, beautiful carpets, and wall decorations had been smashed, shredded, and bitten in half by the gorgons. Aleric could smell their stench from where he stood. A few drops of blood colored the white carpet near the door.

"She's gone," Dartan said. He leaned against the door, his face paler than usual. "We failed."

"Who's gone?"

The vampire and werewolf turned to see Vallia standing on the steps behind them.

"If you're here, who did they take?" Dartan asked. He leaned down and touched one of the drops of blood. He brought it to his lips and tasted it.

"It's human," he said with dread in his voice.

"Lilian," Aleric whispered.

Everyone followed his gaze. On the ground near the door lay a single white rose, its petals crushed and bruised against the carpet as though it had been stepped on by a heavy foot. Half of the rose was red. Aleric didn't have to pick the rose up to know that the color was blood.

"They'll pay for this," Dartan said.

Aleric phased into wolf form and ran back out the door.

About the Author

Cheree Alsop is an award-winning, best-selling author who has published over 35 books, including two series through Stonehouse Ink. She is the mother of a beautiful, talented daughter and amazing twin sons who fill every day with joy and laughter. She is married to her best friend, Michael, the light of her life and her soulmate who shares her dreams and inspires her by reading the first drafts and giving much appreciated critiques. Cheree works as a fulltime author and mother, which is more play than work! She enjoys reading, traveling to tropical beaches, riding motorcycles, spending time with her wonderful children, and going on family adventures while planning her next book.

Cheree and Michael live in Utah where they rock out, enjoy the outdoors, plan great quests, and never stop dreaming.

Look for Dr. Wolf, the Fae Rift Series, Book 4- Dragon's Bayne. It will be available October 2016.

To be added to Cheree's email list for notification of book releases, please send her an email to chereelalsop@hotmail.com

You can find Cheree's other books at www.chereealsop.com

If you enjoyed this book, please review it so that others will be able to share in the adventure!

REVIEWS

The Girl from the Stars Series

This is my favorite Cheree Alsop book now! Her best yet! I loved it. So many twists and turns, great characters, excitement and hints of romance. I can't wait for the next one in the series.
—Voca Matisse, Reviewer

Fantastic book! Cheree's ability to write an amazing character that you not only sympathize with but also grow to care for, is one of the fabulous writing abilities that she lends to every story. This story line was full of epic twists and wry humor that had me engaged the entire way through. All in all a fun enjoyable read.
—akgodwin, Amazon Reviewer

This was one of the best books I have read in a while. Sci-fyi, adventure, thriller... could not put the book away. I already bought the second book in the series, and hope the third will come out soon.
—Kindle Customer

The main character, Liora, is a very mixed up but emerging person who is a genetic mutt! Half of her DNA is totally violence oriented whilst the other half is straight human, which is to say violent when necessary but basically well rounded. In the beginning she was a slave in a circus and had never known anyone she could trust or care for, and even when she is rescued from that hell she has a hard time adjusting to the idea that she can fit in anywhere. The action is frequent and well written and over time she keeps trying to both find reasons to fit in and reasons to strike out on her own. This is not resolved in the first book, and makes you want to read more. I like the series a lot and hope the writer keeps them coming.

—Sam, Amazon Reviewer

The Silver Series

"Cheree Alsop has written *Silver* for the YA reader who enjoys both werewolves and coming-of-age tales. Although I don't fall into this demographic, I still found it an entertaining read on a long plane trip! The author has put a great deal of thought into balancing a tale that could apply to any teen (death of a parent, new school, trying to find one's place in the world) with the added spice of a youngster dealing with being exceptionally different from those around him, and knowing that puts him in danger."

—Robin Hobb, author of the Farseer Trilogy

"I honestly am amazed this isn't absolutely EVERYWHERE! Amazing book. Could NOT put it down! After reading this book, I purchased the entire series!"

—Josephine, Amazon Reviewer

"A page-turner that kept me wide awake and wanting more. Great characters, well written, tenderly developed, and thrilling. I loved this book, and you will too."

—Valerie McGilvrey

"Super glad that I found this series! I am crushed that it is at its end. I am sure we will see some of the characters in the next series, but it just won't be the same. I am 41 years old, and am only a little embarrassed to say I was crying at 3 a.m. this morning while finishing the last book. Although this is a YA series, all ages will enjoy the Silver Series. Great job by Cheree Alsop. I am excited to see what she comes up with next."

—Jennc, Amazon Reviewer

The Werewolf Academy Series

If you love werewolves, paranormal, and looking for a book like House of Night or Vampire Academy this is it! YA for sure.

—Reviewer for Sweets Books

I got this book from a giveaway, and it's one of the coolest books I have ever read. If you love Hogwarts, and Vampire Academy, or basically anything that has got to do with supernatural people studying, this is the book for you.

—Maryam Dinzly

This series is truly a work of art, sucked in immediately and permanently. The first line and you are in the book. Cheree Alsop is a gifted writer, all of her books are my complete favorites!! This series has to be my absolute favorite, Alex is truly a wonderful character who I so wish was real so I can meet him and thank him. Once you pick this book up you won't put it down till it's finished. A must read!!!!!

—BookWolf Brianna

Listed with Silver Moon as the top most emotional of Cheree's books, I loved Instinct for its raw truth about the pain, the heartbreak, and the guilt that Alex fights.
—Loren Weaver

Great story. Loaded with adventure at every turn. Can't wait till the next book. Very enjoyable, light reading. I would recommend to all young and old readers.
—Sharon Klein

The Galdoni Series

"This is absolutely one of the best books I have ever read in my life! I loved the characters and their personalities, the storyline and the way it was written. The bravery, courage and sacrifice that Kale showed was amazing and had me scolding myself to get a grip and stop crying! This book had adventure, romance and comedy all rolled into one terrific book I LOVED the lesson in this book, the struggles that the characters had to go through (especially the forbidden love)...I couldn't help wondering what it would be like to live among such strangely beautiful creatures that acted, at times, more caring and compassionate than the humans. Overall, I loved this book...I recommend it to ANYONE who fancies great books."
—iBook Reviewer

"I was not expecting a free novel to beat anything that I have ever laid eyes upon. This book was touching and made me want more after each sentence."
—Sears1994, iBook Reviewer

"This book was simply heart wrenching. It was an amazing book with a great plot. I almost cried several times. All of the scenes were so real it felt like I was there witnessing everything."
—Jeanine Drake, iBook Reveiwer

"Galdoni is an amazing book; it is the first to actually make me cry! It is a book that really touches your heart, a romance novel that might change the way you look at someone. It did that to me."
—Coralee2, Reviewer

"Wow. I simply have no words for this. I highly recommend it to anyone who stumbled across this masterpiece. In other words, READ IT!"
—Troublecat101, iBook Reviewer

The Monster Asylum Series

What a rollercoaster, wow!! I never ever cried when reading a vampire book, but I did this time. I must say it's the best vampire book I've read since ever. One of the best books ever read so far.
—Conny, Goodreads Reviewer

I downloaded this book because of Cheree, I love her imagination. This one is so much fun to read,once I started I couldn't put it down. And now I believe not all Monsters are bad!! Looking forward to the next book in the series. Thanks Cheree
—Doughgirl61, Amazon Reviewer

Keeper of the Wolves

"This is without a doubt the VERY BEST paranormal romance/adventure I have ever read and I've been reading these types of books for over 45 years. Excellent plot, wonderful protagonists—even the evil villains were great. I read this in one sitting on a Saturday morning when there were so many other things I should have been doing. I COULD NOT put it down! I also appreciated the author's research and insights into the behavior of wolf packs. I will CERTAINLY read more by this author and put her on my 'favorites' list."

—N. Darisse

"This is a novel that will emotionally cripple you. Be sure to keep a box of tissues by your side. You will laugh, you will cry, and you will fall in love with Keeper. If you loved *Black Beauty* as a child, then you will truly love *Keeper of the Wolves* as an adult. Put this on your 'must read' list."

—Fortune Ringquist

"Cheree Alsop mastered the mind of a wolf and wrote the most amazing story I've read this year. Once I started, I couldn't stop reading. Personal needs no longer existed. I turned the last page with tears streaming down my face."

—Rachel Andersen, Amazon Reviewer

"I just finished this book. Oh my goodness, did I get emotional in some spots. It was so good. The courage and love portrayed is amazing. I do recommend this book. Thought provoking."

—Candy, Amazon Reviewer

Thief Prince

"I absolutely loved this book! I could not put it down. . . The Thief Prince will whisk you away into a new world that you will not want to leave! I hope that Ms. Alsop has more about this story to write, because I would love more Kit and Andric! This is one of my favorite books so far this year! Five Stars!"
—Crystal, Book Blogger at Books are Sanity

". . . Once I started I couldn't put it down. The story is amazing. The plot is new and the action never stops. The characters are believable and the emotions presented are beautiful and real. If anyone wants a good, clean, fun, romantic read, look no further. I hope there will be more books set in Debria, or better yet, Antor."
—SH Writer, Amazon Reviewer

"This book was a roller coaster of emotions: tears, laughter, anger, and happiness. I absolutely fell in love with all of the characters placed throughout this story. This author knows how to paint a picture with words."
—Kathleen Vales

"Awesome book! It was so action packed, I could not put it down, and it left me wanting more! It was very well written, leaving me feeling like I had a connection with the characters."
—M. A., Amazon Reviewer

The Shadows Series

"This was a heart-warming tale of rags to riches. It was also wonderfully described and the characters were vivid and vibrant; a story that teaches of love defying boundaries and of people finding acceptance."
—Sara Phillip, Book Reviewer

"This is the best book I have ever had the pleasure of reading. . . It literally has everything, drama, action, fighting, romance, adventure, & suspense. . . Nexa is one of the most incredible female protagonists ever written. . .It literally had me on pins & needles the ENTIRE time. . . I cannot recommend this book highly enough. Please give yourself a wonderful treat & read this book... you will NOT be disappointed!!!"
—Jess- Goodreads Reviewer

"Took my breath away; excitement, adventure and suspense. . . This author has extracted a tender subject and created a supernatural fantasy about seeing beyond the surface of an individual. . . Also the romantic scenes would make a girl swoon. . . The fights between allies and foes and blood lust would attract the male readers. . .The conclusion was so powerful and scary this reader was sitting on the edge of her seat."
—Susan Mahoney, Book Blogger

"Adventure, incredible amounts of imagination and description go into this world! It is a buy now, don't leave the couch until the last chapter has reached an end kind of read!"
—Malcay- Amazon Reviewer

"The high action tale with the underlying love story that unfolds makes you want to keep reading and not put it down. I can't wait until the next book in the Shadows Series comes out."

—Karen- Amazon Reviewer

". . . It's refreshing to see a female character portrayed without the girly cliches most writers fall into. She is someone I would like to meet in real life, and it is nice to read the first person POV of a character who is so well-round that she is brave, but still has the softer feminine side that defines her character. A definite must read."

—S. Teppen- Goodreads Reviewer

The Small Town Superhero Series

"A very human superhero- Cheree Alsop has written a great book for youth and adults alike. Kelson, the superhero, is battling his own demons plus bullies in this action packed narrative. Small Town Superhero had me from the first sentence through the end. I felt every sorrow, every pain and the delight of rushing through the dark on a motorcycle. Descriptions in Small Town Superhero are so well written the reader is immersed in the town and lives of its inhabitants."

—Rachel Andersen, Book Reviewer

"Anyone who grew up in a small town or around motorcycles will love this! It has great characters and flows well with martial arts fighting and conflicts involved."

—Karen, Amazon Reviewer

"Fantastic story...and I love motorcycles and heroes who don't like the limelight. Excellent character development. You'll like this series!"
—Michael, Amazon Reviewer

"Another great read; couldn't put it down. Would definitely recommend this book to friends and family. She has put out another great read. Looking forward to reading more!"
—Benton Garrison, Amazon Reviewer

"I enjoyed this book a lot. Good teen reading. Most books I read are adult contemporary; I needed a change and this was a good change. I do recommend reading this book! I will be looking out for more books from this author. Thank you!"
—Cass, Amazon Reviewer

Stolen

"This book will take your heart, make it a little bit bigger, and then fill it with love. I would recommend this book to anyone from 10-100. To put this book in words is like trying to describe love. I had just gotten it and I finished it the next day because I couldn't put it down. If you like action, thrilling fights, and/or romance, then this is the perfect book for you."
—Steven L. Jagerhorn

"Couldn't put this one down! Love Cheree's ability to create totally relatable characters and a story told so fluidly you actually believe it's real."

—Sue McMillin, Amazon Reviewer

"I enjoyed this book it was exciting and kept you interested. The characters were believable. And the teen romance was cute."
—Book Haven- Amazon Reviewer

"I really liked this book . . . I was pleasantly surprised to discover this well-written book. . .I'm looking forward to reading more from this author."
—Julie M. Peterson- Amazon Reviewer

"Great book! I enjoyed this book very much it keeps you wanting to know more! I couldn't put it down! Great read!"
—Meghan- Amazon Reviewer

"A great read with believable characters that hook you instantly. . . I was left wanting to read more when the book was finished."
—Katie- Goodreads Reviewer

Heart of the Wolf

"Absolutely breathtaking! This book is a roller coaster of emotions that will leave you exhausted!!! A beautiful fantasy filled with action and love. I recommend this book to all fantasy lovers and those who enjoy a heartbreaking love story that rivals that of Romeo and Juliet. I couldn't put this book down!"
—Amy May

"What an awesome book! A continual adventure, with surprises on every page. What a gifted author she is. You just can't put the book down. I read it in two days. Cheree has a way of developing relationships and pulling at your heart. You find yourself identifying with the characters in her book...True life situations make this book come alive for you and gives you increased understanding of your own situation in life. Magnificent story and characters. I've read all of Cheree's books and recommend them all to you...especially if you love adventures."
—Michael, Amazon Reviewer

"You'll like this one and want to start part two as soon as you can! If you are in the mood for an adventure book in a faraway kingdom where there are rival kingdoms plotting and scheming to gain more power, you'll enjoy this novel. The characters are well developed, and of course with Cheree there is always a unique supernatural twist thrown into the story as well as romantic interests to make the pages fly by."
Karen, Amazon Reviewer

When Death Loved an Angel

"This style of book is quite a change for this author so I wasn't expecting this, but I found an interesting story of two very different souls who stepped outside of their "accepted roles" to find love and forgiveness, and what is truly of value in life and death."
—Karen, Amazon Reviewer

"When Death Loved an Angel by Cheree Alsop is a touching paranormal romance that cranks the readers' thinking mode into high gear."

—Rachel Andersen, Book Reviewer

"Loved this book. I would recommend this book to everyone. And be sure to check out the rest of her books, too!"

—Malcay, Book Reviewer

The Million Dollar Gift

…This was a very beautiful, heart warming story about a young man who finds love, and family again on Christmas. I really enjoyed this short story. It truly inspires the meaning of Christmas in my eyes. It was utterly beautiful, and I highly recommend it. The plot is very interesting, and the characters catch your heart and lead on this very sad and happy story.

—Whitney@Shooting Stars Review

I recommend The Million Dollar Gift as a way to remember what Christmas is about: Love. Family. Friendship. Because a life without love isn't really worth living anyway.

—Loren Weaver

When Chase risks his life to save a brother and sister just before Christmas, his life becomes entwined with theirs more intricately than he could have imagined. Emotional and moving, this is a story of a young man whose troubled heart is tested by the one thing he is unprepared to face, love. MY TAKE- This is a fast, fun, emotional Christmas read. Made me cry.

—Donna Weaver

Never stop dreaming!

Made in the USA
Coppell, TX
10 March 2021